2

M Y STORY STARTS with two bodies. The first is right here in front of me, tucked between white sheets. The other is sprawled out on the polished floor of a convention centre in Moscow, a lifetime ago.

It is, I suppose, slightly misleading to call them bodies. They're not dead. Not yet.

I should tell you where I am.

I'm in the master bedroom of a house. The same bedroom of the same house that I have occupied for the past fifty years. Around me are the people that – for better or for worse – I have come to call my family. It is morning.

Jessica is holding her granddad's hand. It's a simple gesture – her dainty fist closed around his knotted fingers – but I would give anything to spend ten seconds in her place now, to feel his fading warmth. I have always longed for the fluency of touch.

The fact is, I think Roger is going to die today. And it's with this in mind that we'll need to return to that other body, to balance the scale. So let's go back to the exhibition centre in Moscow, 1959.

In a dome in Sokol'niki Park a cultural exchange was taking place. The dome was stuffed with Americana: kitchen appliances and muscle cars. Roger was there to meet a friend.

In one section of the exhibition there was a film playing on repeat. It opened with a narrator purring over images of the night sky, a vision of celestial unity. Then there were rows on rows of clapboard houses, shot from above, with picket fences on the front lawns and swimming pools in the gardens, cut with shots of the Grand Canyon, the Rocky Mountains. The great American West.

Groups of comrades were bussed in from the factories. They were given the tour, shown a microwave and a vacuum cleaner. They sat behind the wheel of a Cadillac. But really they were there to find faults. The Americans had come to tell a story, but the Soviets wanted to tell one of their own.

At the centre of it all was a collection of American art, curated to showcase the best works of the preceding three decades. Stark paintings of the frontier were hung next to canvases exploding with colour and shape.

There was one painting that was particularly popular. It depicted a high society dinner in a New York banqueting hall. Yellow was dominant, from the half-empty glasses of champagne to the silk crepe of a dowager's elaborate ball gown, giving the whole scene a jaundiced hue. The chair of the American selection committee had wanted to have it removed. The title of the painting was *Welcome Home*, and it was in front of this painting that Roger had arranged to meet his friend.

Now I've started telling this story, I don't know that I'll ever be able to stop. The details pile up. My pages will grow and grow until they plaster the walls and the windows – until they block out the light. This room will become a perfect simulacrum of my mind.

Remembering that day in 1959 is lending a new sharpness to objects in the present. On the table beside Roger's bed there is a drawing in a little clip frame. Jessica drew it for Roger when she was barely out of nappies, in a period when she and her mother were staying here. It's the typical scene, two stick figures beside a house. There are marshmallow clouds and a sun smiling down from one corner. At the bottom, below the house and the figures, the words 'Jess and Grandpa' are spelled out in uncertain letters. It's a scene that almost every child draws for their parents or grandparents – one of the first stories that children learn to tell. The one about the house and the family. The one about home.

Next to the drawing, in an older, more elaborate frame is a sepia photograph of Margery herself. She would have been only a few years older than Jessica is today when it was taken. The hair is different, and the nose, but the eyes are unmistakable.

Beside the table sits Ruth: Jessica's mother, Margery's daughter. She's clutching a small, calf-bound volume. Holding it to her chest, just over her heart.

It's one of those books that doesn't seem to exist until it's needed, until these moments of original fear when faith – inborn and subliminal – rises to the surface. The accumulated legacy of faith – that's the comfort it brings. It's a book that has presided over weddings and funerals, baptisms and confirmations. It connects the dots between Ruth and her antecedents and the moments they themselves groped for the eternal. It's freighted with their joy and their terror.

I should know. I've spent more time as a family bible than anyone.

Roger and his friend wanted to meet somewhere busy in Moscow that day, so as to draw less attention. A crowd in which they could lose any surveillance.

Is this what success looks like to you? the man asked

5

Roger, staring up at the decadent scene before him. As he spoke two grey-looking men approached through the crowd.

Roger was saying something about the gaucheness of American money, but I had stopped listening. They laughed and just as Roger's friend turned to reply, one of the men bumped into him.

Within a couple of seconds the first man had disappeared into the crowd, trailing a mumbled apology. The smile froze on Roger's friend's face as his hand went to his thigh and then to his chest. He blinked once and I watched as a new dawn, one of terror, broke across his face. He began to fall, and at that moment the second man arrived to catch him.

We need to get something straight. I am not the average storyteller – and mine is not the average story.

As we go on you may find it strange that I presume to *know* Roger. I don't just mean in the way that a mother might know a child, or a husband his wife. More than that. I can make the speculative leap between his actions and his thoughts.

But the fact is, I do. I know the lineage of these actions, the forgotten ancestors of each twitch and affectation. I was there at the conception of each habit and at the birth of each desire. I have watched, and I have watched, and I have watched. Accusations of arrogance would be misplaced. There is no place for pride in this: the quiet accumulation of the minutiae of a human life.

My love for him defies the usual categories. It is a klepto-maniacal passion for each thread of his history. The collection and preservation of these threads has been the great work of my love, which fuels and defines it.

But I apologise. How remiss of me. I didn't finish. I am

getting to be rather old myself, you see. So yes, you may find it strange when I tell you that, as Roger watched a bead of sweat trace a line down his friend's forehead, as this friend was carried away by a man who – miraculously – arrived to catch him before he had even begun to fall, Roger's mind was somewhere else. Slowly receding through the crowd, he was thinking of another story, one about a monastery in a far-flung place, and of the terrible things that had happened there.

As to what he's thinking here and now, I couldn't guess. Even I can't follow the thread into that twilight land.

It has been over fifty years since that day in the convention centre, but it seems a fitting event with which to begin the telling of this story, which is now drawing to a close.

If go back to the newspapers for that day in 1959, in one of the tabloids you will find a photo. It shows a man in a Colonel's uniform in a dead faint, being carried away by another man with bovine eyes, under the headline YANKEE ART PROVES TOO MUCH FOR THE REDS. In the background you can see Roger, looking in horror at his friend, his body half-turned to disappear into the crowd. If you look very closely, you'll see me, poking out of the left top pocket of his blazer. I should introduce myself.

My name is John, and I am this book.

3

OFTEN, WHEN A place is very familiar, it becomes difficult to recall the ways in which it has changed.

It's a problem of aspect. From my viewpoint here on top of the bookshelf, it's hard for me to see the room any way other than how it is today – the way it has been for perhaps the last fifteen years.

I see Roger. I see the bed.

But if I imagine myself plucked from the shelf by an invisible hand and placed at Roger's side, then, all of a sudden, the years fall away.

I look up and find that a point which had seemed merely a slight discolouration in the paintwork – perhaps a trick of the light – is in fact a shallow crater in the plaster. It's an inch deep, a couple of inches across.

This room hasn't always been Roger's bedroom. It was the day that I came to the house, and it is again now, but for a while it belonged to his daughter Ruth.

Ruth had been furious, in the beetroot-faced way that only toddlers and the criminally insane can be. It hardly matters what for. But it was the wall of this room that felt the full force of her fury, transferred through the corner of a red building block by Ruth's surprisingly strong throwing arm.

From the bed I'm now swept by that same invisible hand to the floor, peeling back another ten years. I'm on the loose floorboard, the one that would groan every time adolescent

Roger turned in his sleep. Silenced for the years that – carpeted in pea-green pile – it served as Ruth's nursery, it groans again now as Jess leans forward out of her chair to sweep Roger's limp fringe from his face.

And with that moment of tenderness the years restratify and compress. The invisible hand places me back on the shelf.

This room bears witness, as I do. It cannot do otherwise. And that is because, like me, it has no direct say in its aspect – in the way that it stands in relation to the years that pass over it.

I'm being circumspect. My imagination isn't my only transport; I might not be able to move, but I can change.

Let me explain: I met Roger on a bus.

I began that day[1] in the house of a filing clerk in whose dour company I had seen out the Blitz. I had been trying everything to induce him to slip me into his briefcase so that I might make my escape. When he caught sight of me that morning on the kitchen table, while eating his toast, it was with some surprise. He had left me the night before as an entirely different book.[2]

I hate toast. I really do. The crumbs get caught between your pages and then slip down to your gatherings. Like a stone in your shoe, one wet with saliva. So spare a thought, toast munchers. Have some compassion.

There was something about that book, perhaps the seductively bold red-on-black dust wrapper, which made it

1 Agatha Christie, *The Body in the Library* (Collins: London, 1942) – rather obvious, I know.
2 Keith Feiling, *The Life of Neville Chamberlain* (Macmillan & Co: London, 1946) – Bill looked for things in the childhoods of great men that matched his own to try to convince himself that his insignificance was an accident of circumstance. He liked a good dose of bitter self-recrimination with his Horlicks.

irresistible to Bill. As he was passing the table on his way to the door he paused and I found myself plunged into his briefcase. My spine came to rest against a spam sandwich.

When he opened up his case on the bus he became frantic – his pristine copy of the Christie was nowhere to be found. In his frustration he left the copy of that week's *Spectator*[3] – which had mysteriously found its way into his briefcase – on the seat next to him.

I was snapped up by a leather-gloved hand and found myself confronted by a puffy face caked with powder, framed by a tartan nylon hood. This woman read my cover disdainfully. Then, to my disgust, she removed one of her gloves and licked her finger before turning my pages. I've made my thoughts about saliva clear.

I was powerless to do anything when she rang the bell and rolled me up, stuffing me into her handbag as she breezed past the conductor and out onto the street. Nelson's column loomed above.

Now I was in a predicament. As a rule, I avoid going coverless. It's risky, it makes me ephemeral and disposable. I had gone out on a limb that day because I was bored and desperate. And now, not only was I coverless, I was also at the mercy of the elements. You see, books are indoor creatures by necessity – we're made of frailer stuff than flesh.

Exempting, of course, when we're made from flesh.

I tried it once – anthropodermic biblioplegy. Though

---

3   *Spectator* (14th March, 1947) – the book of the day was a biography of Thomas Paine, who famously wrote that, 'Natural rights are those which appertain to man in right of his existence.' Life and liberty being foremost. Having just escaped imprisonment myself – and in light of the disputable nature of my 'existence' – I had my reservations about whether this was an auspicious coincidence.

I suppose what I did would be autoanthropodermic biblioplegy.

I'm being drawn irresistibly sideways. Hold onto the woman with the forlorn magazine poking out of her handbag for a moment - we'll come back to her. If this is to be a chapter of changes then this will be instructive.

My transmogrification into human flesh was a much earlier, aborted, attempt at setting myself down: an unmitigated disaster. Dressing that way attracts entirely the wrong crowd.

I thought I would try out being a found text. I'd write an entirely new book, engineer a situation where I would be discovered and hey presto! I would announce myself. I wanted something headline grabbing. My first thought was a heretical pamphlet, but that would only have caught the attention of a certain kind of reader. Then I thought perhaps something on divorce - it worked pretty well for Milton.

When the solution came, it hit me like a bolt of horrible brilliance: a murder confession.

The binding of this book is made from the flayed skin of John Roberts, at his request.

The autoanthropodermy was ancillary to the main idea, it just seemed neat for the murderer's confession to be bound in his own skin. It was uncomfortable - scratchy. Human skin doesn't tan well, not nearly so well as vellum. It is thin and brittle and curls up at the corners.

I want to beg the forgiveness of God for the things which I here do confess. I murdered my wife, Eleanor Roberts, in the heat of a jealous passion and it is my wish that this confession be bound up in my own skin as a penance for the barbarous crime that I visited upon her. I am soon to be hanged for these crimes and while I await my fate it is my desire to tell my story to the chaplain of this gaol so that my story may be a warning to others who

Once I got started I just couldn't stop.

I took my style queues from the handbills published by the Ordinary of Newgate. Supposedly responsible for the spiritual care of the condemned, he sold their 'confessions' for sixpence at executions.

John Roberts gave me the release that I had been looking for; he was the empty cup into which I poured all of my impotent rage and frustration, shored up in my pages through centuries of passive immobility, to give this newfound agency the name of action.

I had him sleeping, eating, drinking. I had him fishing and chopping wood. I craved anything physical. The majority of the account covered the summer running up to the murder of his wife, spent tramping through East Anglia looking for farm work. While there was call for Eleanor as a milker, John's hands were rough and unschooled. Every place they stopped at he was told there was nothing for him until harvest. John would sleep rough while he waited for Eleanor, drinking away her wages.

What started out as a murder confession evolved into a pantheistic tract. It was those days and nights that he spent alone in the woods and fields that gave me licence to inhabit him fully and, through him, to occupy the world that I was creating around him. When it came to describing the act itself, which took place in a poky room above an inn near Cambridge, I took scant pleasure. I cursed myself for picking a conceit that demanded such a swift conclusion, though having a defined, parenthetical structure within which to explore my selfhood was reassuring.

I made no attempt at covering my tracks or obscuring details. Part of me has always wanted to get caught.

At that time I was situated in the house of a banker on Cheapside – Nathan Mayer Rothschild. He was straightening his papers, getting ready to go out for the evening, when he came across me. He opened me up and his eyes went immediately to the inscription. He read it once, then again, before dropping me back onto the table. His raised his hands to the ceiling in horror.

However, it wasn't horror that showed itself in his eyes, but curiosity. Tentatively, his hands snaked back towards me. When he picked me up it was with his fingertips, but as he turned the first page he licked his lips. And that's when I knew that I had him. He forgot about his plans for that evening entirely and sat and read on into the night.

My thirst for experience had led to a text over-abundant in mundane detail. Rothschild lapped it up. People never want to see evil in a great black shroud, carrying a sickle. No. You want to see it with its trousers down as the outhouse door swings open in the breeze.

And there's the sweet horror of it, that closeness, the possibility you feel just under the skin, imagining for a moment that it could have been you. That's what I was looking for. As Rothschild's bilious, bloated face floated above me, filled with excitement – that's what I wanted to feel: that I might reach out and choke the life out of him.

It was curiosity, of a different order entirely, that attracted me to Roger. As I mentioned, I met him on a bus.

Let's return to the lady with the tartan nylon hood, and to where we left her, standing by the bus stop in Trafalgar Square. And I, stuffed into her handbag, fearing my own destruction.

She didn't move far. I slipped into the depths of her handbag, ensconced in a frilly handkerchief scented with lavender. It's a scent that always makes me think of corpses – of masked rottenness.

By the time the lady opened her bag and pulled me out I found that I was on a bus once more.[4] For her part, the lady was astonished to find that – instead of a copy of the *Spectator* – she held a copy of a rather saucy nautical romance in her hand. Surprise didn't inspire a more endearing configuration of her facial features than had contempt, so I was glad when she put me down on the seat in front of her.

I hardly had a moment to congratulate myself on another lucky escape before someone sat down beside me, dropping a bag on top of me and plunging me into darkness.

A moment more and I felt the bag lifted from my cover and there he was. There was Roger.

His hair was wet with the rain; there were droplets caught in the fine hairs of his eyebrows. As he scanned my cover, he licked his lips.

4 Constance Wellspring, *The Adventures of Captain Lionhard* (Kidd & Co.: London, 1938) – you won't find a copy of this book in the catalogues of the British Library. Or, in fact, anywhere at all. It was a salacious little romance that I would amuse myself with in quiet moments and – forced to think fast – it was the first thing that came to the page. I was particularly proud of the cover, a buxom mermaid wrapped around a grounded ship's anchor. Improbable sexual encounters have always been a special interest of mine.

That's when I knew I had him. It's how I always know.

He looked around for whomever had left me, his eyes coming to rest on those of the lady sitting behind. His face reddened with the heat of her disapproval before breaking, suddenly, into a disarming smile.

'I'm so sorry, is this book yours?'

That seemed to settle things. He took me up, opening me up to my first page. Now I had my first real chance to study his face.

I'm rather an expert in faces. I've spent a good deal of time staring up at them. Roger's, at first glance, was unremarkable. But this characterisation was a result of that dullness brought about by familiarity that I have already discussed, a fault of aspect. And as I looked past it – past his square jaw, his slightly bulbous nose – I began to see those artefacts that were its real character.

There was the thin, hooked scar that trailed from his left eyebrow to the base of his eye-socket: over-reaching for some fruitcake as a toddler. Then there were the fine lines radiating from the corners of his mouth, which appeared when he pursed his lips in concentration. His history was there, to be read in his features, but at that point they were meaningless signs.

Fifteen pages on, the heat was returning to Roger's cheeks. He looked up and wiped condensation from window, before ringing the bell and stuffing me in his bag.

We had arrived at his family home, a town house off the Northcote Road. The blackout curtains still hung in the window, in fresh remembrance of the Blitz. We were greeted by his mother.

'Roger, is that you?' She thundered down the stairs. 'Where on God's green earth have you been?'

She had come out from her bedroom onto the landing, I could tell by the wafting smell of cigarette smoke. Though I did not see her that first day, I always remember her like that, with a cigarette hanging from her creased lips. Roger said nothing and I felt the satchel bump against her hips as he bustled past.

I tumbled out of Roger's satchel and he kicked me under the bed. I heard the springs creak in response to his weight above me. After a while I heard his mother's voice, calling from somewhere below the floorboards on which I lay. Roger let out a sigh, echoed by the bedsprings as he rolled out of bed and out of the room.

And so I had a little pause in which to review my change in fortune.

The shadows grew and swung themselves across the surface of Roger's bedroom floor, chased by the orange, dying day. Then it was dark. Which was fine. I'm quite used to it. No one ever thinks to leave the lights on for me. Eventually, through the yawning dark I heard the door click, groan, click close again, and felt flecks of dust floating down onto my cover, displaced from the springs by Roger's weight.

The loose floorboard, on which I lay, creaked. His hand groped around until it fell upon me.

He read me cover to cover in the thin electric light. The next day and the next night were the same; as the days drew on he began to work out which bits he particularly wanted to read and started skipping to them. Getting straight to the heavy breathing.

I spent the days listening and learning. I listened to the footsteps of Roger's mother, Joan, as she pottered around the kitchen in the morning, letting her family know that London was waking by creating a din entirely disproportionate to the business of egg frying. I listened to the return of his father Philip from work, his satisfied sighs as he slid his feet out of his leather shoes in the master bedroom, and the clink and splash of the whisky decanter as he poured himself a drink. I listened to the creaking of the ailing lead pipes and the patter of the oak branches as they advanced and retreated against Roger's window. I stored up these little waymarkers and by them built a patchwork picture of the house and the daily lives of its inhabitants.

Roger's interest dwindled. After a couple of months he stopped reading me altogether. By the time that his exasperated mother pulled me out from under the bed in one of her whirlwind attacks on Roger's room, I was ready to be discovered[5]. She picked me up and placed me on the bookshelf that I sit on now. That night I watched him sleep, as I do now.

You'll have to forgive me my digressions. My thoughts follow a logic more associative than chronological. Who is really interested in the order that things happen? It's the reasons that matter. In the end, they are what we remember.

5 Charles Dickens, *Oliver Twist* (OUP: Oxford, 1938) – no parent can possibly object to Dickens.

4

ROGER HAD HIS first stroke two years ago.

It was just after four in the afternoon. I remember because *Countdown* was on. I'm very good at *Countdown*. It seems a shame that I'll never be able to apply to be a contestant.

In the middle of a very satisfying 'letters' round, the left side of Roger's face began to sag. This, to me, was not such a remarkable thing – I thought that he might be asleep, and sleep does seem to inflict all manner of bizarre arrangements on people's facial features. What alerted me to the fact that something was wrong was that the other side of his face gradually folded itself up into a mask of terror.

Nothing happened for two very long minutes, after which Roger was able to raise a palsied hand to the telephone which he kept on the table next to his armchair. After getting through to the ambulance service, he managed to struggle his way through the address, a tragic parody of a thin-lipped Hollywood gangster.

The paramedics came, unfolded him on to a stretcher, and stole him away from my view – howling off down the road under the hail of sirens. He was gone for six days. You can't begin to imagine the amount of anxiety that is shored up over six days in an empty house. People make so much noise simply being: the little grunts and sighs that punctuate the interminable business of breathing, the susurrations of fabric moving over fabric and skin that accompany every tiny readjustment of the body. Sound pursues you everywhere, and it makes the silence that drops like a curtain in your absence so profound. I have always found my inability to break this silence excruciating. I can't count the times I have longed for a throat to clear.

The stroke happened so suddenly, and was such an undramatic – almost apologetic – attempt on his life, that I couldn't possibly imagine him actually *dying* as a result of it. On the evening of the sixth day a car rattled to a halt in front of the house. I heard the sound of the front door opening and closing, the clumsy scuffling of feet: he'd made it. The old fool was still alive.

There is no denying that it was a turning point. When he limped back into this room, leaning heavily on the arm of a nurse, his whole manner was changed. His face had fallen into lines of defeat and, once we were left alone, tears settled into dew on the soft hairs of his chin.

Growing up doesn't seem to be half as hard as growing old. Both are marked by tears and confusion, but for the old the tears fall unheeded, and the confusion thickens with time.

Not only is his old body diminishing, but the space that he inhabits is contracting around him too. His world has receded into this room. And as his universe has got smaller, mine has too. I haven't moved an inch since he came back from the hospital. We've stayed together, bathed by the tides of our private reflections.

It was around that time that Jessica started coming to visit. Before that she would come, birthdays and holidays, but it was incidental – she was always on her way to somewhere else. After the stroke she stopped glancing at the clock.

She would sneak around downstairs, opening and closing cupboards. She developed this bizarre intimation that Roger's nurses were stealing from him, cursing them when she couldn't find his good cups. They weren't, of course; they were consummate professionals, but why let petty fact stand in the way of casting aspersions?

That's unfair. She was right to worry about her granddad; he was growing progressively more vulnerable. What was worse though was his creeping apathy. If the nurses *had* been stealing, he no longer would have been able to find it in himself to care.

It made her angry to see his face swollen with sleep. She wanted him to fight it, to take up tai chi, to drink yoghurt. But there comes a time when everyone decides to stop fighting.

She would make a hell of a racket putting together a sandwich, the noise to ensure that Roger was awake by the time she came upstairs.

To find him sleeping in the middle of the day in his threadbare M&S pyjamas made the fact of his approaching death an unassailable elephant in the room. I enjoyed the clatter and commotion, they reminded me of those mornings when I first came to the house.

It was during one of those visits that she noticed the photo of Margery that Roger keeps by his bed: the sepia portrait in the elaborate frame. She picked it up and studied it, while Roger studied her.

'How old would grandma have been here?'

'It was taken not long after we married. Twenty-three, twenty-four, I suppose?'

'She had such beautiful hair.' Grecian curls, a beauty straight out of a Botticelli painting. I've no idea where it came from. Both her parents were plain as a pikestaff. 'What was she like? When you first married.'

'She was fierce. Bright. And she always knew exactly what she wanted.'

'From you?'

'From everyone and everything. I found that very attractive. She was so sure of herself.'

They were silent a moment, as they both looked at the picture.

'Have I ever told you about the first time we met?' Roger said, and Jessica turned to him. 'It was in Battersea Park in the middle of winter. I was walking with some chaps from the university. We'd just come over the bridge and were about to turn into the park when a little dog darted out through the gates and into the road. Just in front of our feet. Then, right on its heels, a woman came charging through the gates. The dog had shot straight out into the traffic, but she didn't look up. Without thinking, I reached out and grabbed her, and just as I did there was a horrible crunch as the little dog went under the wheels of a car.'

Jessica gasped and brought her hand, in which she still held the little portrait, up to her face. It covered her mouth, confirming the likeness between grandmother's eyes and her own. 'So what happened?'

'She was distraught, of course. It wasn't her dog, it belonged to one of her friends, but she had been holding the lead when the little thing slipped away. It was killed instantly. After we'd sorted out the remains we went for a drink – a little wake – with her friends and my friends. It all seems very morbid now that I'm saying it aloud, but it didn't feel that way.'

'You saved her life. That's a good way of getting a girl's attention.'

Roger smiled. 'I suppose it is. We got talking at the pub and I asked whether I might take her out - to the pictures, I think - and that was that.'

'It's crazy to think that she would only have been a few years older than me when . . . ' She faltered.

Roger took the photo frame from her and smiled once more. 'Look how beautiful she is.'

'Do you mind if I take that photo for a while? I want to make a copy. I'll bring it back after.'

'I don't see why not. Mind you return it though.'

'Promise. And do you have any more photos? Of Grandma.'

'There's a chest of drawers out in the hallway, by the landing. Check the top drawer.'

Jess went out into the hall to bang around and I watched Roger, as he considered his hands. She left soon after, taking a number of photos with her.

It was when he told that story, the one of how he and Margery first met, that I was forced to confront the fact that I was losing him. Taken in its entirety, the story is a lie. But the constituent parts, the details which are strung together to make up the whole, are cannibalised from the actual experience of his life, stripped of their context and reassembled. It's these potted details that give it the ring of truth.

What I couldn't tell was whether this fabrication was accidental or deliberate, whether it was part of a conscious attempt to write his own legacy or simply the product of the stroke - a smudge across the palette of his memories in which certain events had taken on the colour of others. Either way, it served to reinforce my sense of responsibility.

Earlier this morning a nurse came, to clean Roger and turn him to prevent pressure sores. Jessica asked her whether he could still hear her, and the nurse told her that the hearing is always last to go. She didn't tell her the rest: that it'll be the feeling in the hands and feet first, as the nerves spark and misfire, the charge retreating towards the body's core. The bowels will relax; the breathing will slow. But always, right to the very last, Roger will be listening.

She just told Jessica and Ruth to keep speaking to him. And now that Roger is silent, I'll speak too. I'll tell you the story of how they really met.

5

THEY MET ON an autumn afternoon, the golden kind that makes you feel nostalgic for no good reason. Roger was in his second year of university, studying Russian at University College London, and he was sitting in a pub on Fleet Street waiting for a friend.

I was lying in his open satchel on the sticky beer-stained table, and he had his nose buried in another book. There was a wireless in the corner playing the third programme. A Liszt piano concerto.

The frantic chromatics were apt because courtship has always been hard for me to follow. It has its own language, written onto and out of the body, of blood rising to the skin, to spell out that thing which words leave to evaporate in cliché's runnels: the body's ancient intention, expressed as if for the first time. The language of intimacy has no words, yet desire still makes itself understood. Or so I must infer, from the results. My skin does not allow me to join the conversation.

For a long time, when marriage was a transaction between two families, it was simpler: means and ends. But now that these means are an end in themselves my limitations have become more problematic.

Margery noticed Roger first. Or, I spotted Margery noticing Roger. She was sitting with a group of friends, glancing around the pub as she half-listened to a boorish young man telling a story until her eyes came to rest on Roger, finding focus, her fingers suddenly busy, tucking her hair behind her ear. As she turned back to the group, one hand cradled the other by her throat.

A young woman in a pub in the middle of the day was still rare enough that Roger should have noticed her, but for two empty pint glasses on the table in front of him.

The young man rounded off his story with a barking laugh. Roger's head snapped towards the sound, a violent movement which suggested he had been falling asleep. Margery turned – her body betraying its awareness of Roger, his stillness – and their eyes met, for a moment. And then a moment more. Then just at the moment that Roger remembered himself, as his pupils contracted and the skin around his eyes creased in frustration at his exposure, just as he was about to bow his head to hide the blood rising to his cheeks, Margery smiled.

Roger was disarmed. The creases unstitched themselves as his lips parted. And before he had time to re-render his features Margery swung the beam of her smile back to the storyteller. Roger was left to grin at her profile.

Margery now embarked on a campaign of ostentatious in-difference. Another of her companions took over, a new story. She straightened up, arching her back and pouting her lips, her hands clasped demurely at her side.

Your move, Roger.

From behind the shield of his fringe he watched Margery as often as his decency (which – being as he was in the full and unctuous throes of late adolescence – was limited) would allow. His eyes combed her back for any evidence of that smile which had evaporated in an instant, trying to reassure himself that he hadn't dreamt it on the two-pint tightrope walk between consciousness and sleep from which he had just tumbled. But there was no reassurance. Her back offered a rebuke, for not taking the opening that the smile had offered, and a challenge, to find a reply.

Perhaps I am giving too much weight to sighs and blushes. Retrospect lends these gestures significance. Bodies are in constant conversation, I observe it all the time; most of it is subconscious, fleeting – forgotten in the time it takes to straighten a skirt or brush off a trouser leg.

Two things:
My body is deliberate.
My body does not forget.

These things perhaps go some way to explain my hawkish fascination with other, less obdurate, bodies, why I place such significance on their accidental gestures.

You see, every word that is written is etched into my being. Every great work and every pulp entertainment, every suicide note and every shopping list – every word is there if I reach for it. The heat of contact does not fade.

I wear these words on my skin like a coat of armour. I have clung to teleology: words that accumulate with a sense of purpose, of progress, instinctively at first, desperately as time went on – so as not to lose myself in the roar.

My flesh itself can change. I can be bound (quarter, case, spiral, saddle stitch, side stitch) or unbound; I can be paper and card, I can be vellum (calf, sheep, goat, human), I can be staples, glue, thread or plastic. And with all of these changes my flesh speaks to you. These changes I make are to draw you to me, that you might pick me up and take me somewhere new.

My skin cannot blush. I have no throat from which to sigh.

But I have one weapon more powerful than either: my scent. The sweet perfume of vanilla and almond that greets you when you lift an old book from the shelf, a smell that triggers a powerful sense of nostalgia that you cannot place.

An effect not unlike that produced by a golden autumn afternoon, such as the one where I have left Margery and Roger on the cusp of meeting for the very first time. They can wait a little longer. Recounting their first meeting is reminding me of another (my doomed, my own, my only – which I'll come to). I'm going to introduce a bloated corpse, with the hope it will cheer me up.

There are other smells that I can produce, in my deliberate attempts to lure curious fingers towards my covers. I can produce the solvent tang of ink and glue that recalls cracking the spine of a new paperback. I can emanate the toasted aroma of warm photocopies. I keep up with the changing times. But the floral musk of vanilla and almonds remains the most reliable; the bouquet of rot and decay occasioned by the slow degradation of my pages.

As with all things where my body is concerned, it is deliberate. I simulate my own destruction in order to draw you near.

Nathan Mayer Rothschild – target of my anthropodermic biblioplegy revenge fantasies – died in 1836, from septicemia: an infection in an abscess which spread to his blood. When he died, his body was already rotten. And when he was buried, in the Brady Street Ashkenazi Cemetery in Whitechapel, I was buried alongside him.

It was an accident. I never intended to spend the rest of my days watching the gradual decomposition of a man that I had despised; but, for better or worse, I have learned a lot at his side. His widow Hannah was sentimental and just as the coffin was closed, I was slipped inside.

It was not unlike being aboard a ship as the coffin was lowered, swaying, hand-over-hand into the ground. Until the first few fistfuls of earth struck the lid of the coffin. Sound receded as the falling earth was muted by its own slow accumulation. Then the silence, and the darkness was absolute.

After a certain period, absolute silence and darkness take on their own texture. There are no referents by which to determine where the darkness ends and you begin. I felt unstitched. Interstitial.

It might be termed my first truly bodily experience, as it was unmediated by other bodies that bear no likeness to my own. No blushes or sighs or clearing throats. Not a whisper of breath. One of those moments that exposes the absurdity of binary oppositions: when an absence is a presence, when a cruelty is a kindness.

Because it's supposedly tortuous, this deprivation, the way it blurs edges and stretches and contracts time. You all need the rub of the world and the traction of the clock to comprehend your existence. I found that I need neither. All I have ever done is wait, so I have learned to mark my own time. A moment can stretch over whole pages, or eternity can come to an end in eight letters.

And I do not need the affirmation of touch. Every written thing – from a child's first attempt to spell out their own name, to their last will and testament – screams I AM. I am made of I am.

The fact of this was all the affirmation I needed, lying on Nathan's slowly decomposing chest. Alone in the formless dark, I started from the beginning. From the text in which I had been ensconced when I first woke, I cycled through every word that I had worn since. I was a whirlwind of ink and glue, of paper and vellum. For the first time I had no possibility of an audience - no one whose tastes I could anticipate and pander to, to induce them to carry me away. But also no one from whom to fear discovery. For the first time my body was entirely my own, not yet to speak, but to exult, in a solipsistic carnival procession, for no one other than myself the simple fact that

I AM.

Sound returned to me slowly - the signature of falling earth but in reverse, gaining clarity - and then all at once, the thump and tear and splinter of wood as an axe struck the coffin. The muted flare of lantern light haloing a masked face was the last thing I saw before Nathan was hoisted from his grave, and me with him. I fell to the ground unnoticed. Nathan was covered with a sack and thrown over the shoulder of the resurrection man who had come to claim him.

I felt a relieved disappointment as I lay there in the dew, under the dim canopy of stars. I was discovered by the gabbai the following morning when he came to check for any signs that would betray his complicity in the previous night's disinterment. I was the first volume of *The Wealth of Nations* (quarto, first edition). I decided to part from Nathan as I had arrived, to confirm the two things I had learned: my body is deliberate. My body does not forget.

Which is why when Margery laughed, at the bar, after Roger made a joke and offered to buy her a drink, I took note. And why, when she touched his arm and tucked her fringe behind her ear as she made her reply, I recorded each movement.

It is in my nature to interpret these inchoate gestures as statements of intent. I suppose it is perverse to question this nature just because of the fact that events have, in this case, borne out their significance.

What are you reading? I read, on her lips, as she pulled that other book from his pocket.

There were many possible futures. That day, there were still many possible Rogers.

But he replied, and the wheels began to turn:
The Idiot.

Margery laughed once more. Her hand lingered on his arm. And that was it.

They set a date for that Friday and she took off to catch her friends. His eyes lingered on the door for a few moments more, and then fell back to the book in his hands.

Unfortunately I didn't manage to get myself brought along when they met up. I did try my very best, mind you, changing myself into what I thought were the guidebooks to seduction – anthologies of love poems and nineteenth-century French novels. The house was full of books even then: his mother was always coming home from church fairs at the weekends with bags full so I knew I wouldn't get caught out. But I guess bringing a book along on a first date was too much even for Roger.

The date must have gone well because Roger met up with her the very next day and from that point they began to see each other at least three or four times a week.

I found out that she was a history of art student at the Courtauld Institute and that, like Roger, she still lived with her parents. She loved to be outside, and so in those first few months of their courtship they spent countless hours walking. They walked through autumn into winter. They watched the last leaves fall in Battersea Park and stamped in the snow around the still-injured streets of South London. They shivered through meagre picnics, put together out of what they could pinch from their parents' ration-strapped pantries – discussing Greene, Dostoevsky, and the contraction of the Empire.

By Christmas no one would have doubted that they were in love. As I watched him sleep, the corners of his mouth would twitch – the suggestion of a smile. To think of it makes me wish that I could dream, just once, just to see what it feels like.

Margery can be put to one side now though. Before I forget, there's another person that you need to meet. Another important stitch to sew.

6

ROGER'S FATHER PHILIP used to insist that every night after dinner the family spent an hour together, sitting in the front room. When I first arrived at the house, while Roger was still in school, he and Philip would play chess.

This hour was the only time Roger spent with his father. Philip was not a man given to displays of affection.

I remember thinking that he must have taught Roger with his eyebrows how to play chess. If the move was good, the eyebrow raise would be slight, and his lower lip would jut out a small amount. If the move was bad, on the other hand, his eyebrows would race upwards to meet his side parting – his eyes searching for something in the corner of the room.

Joan would sit in an armchair by the window pretending to read and firing advice at the pair, which they roundly ignored. This didn't offend or deter her though, and it didn't dispel the domestic contentedness that characterised this part of every evening. Philip would keep a close eye on the mantelpiece clock, and once half an hour had expired he would take up the paper, and the game would be put on hold until the next day.

Roger was a fast learner, and by the time that he got to university he stopped looking up at his father after he had made his moves.

Then one night as I was carried down the stairs, I heard the canned sound of a wireless coming from the front room.

Typically preoccupied, Roger didn't notice until he trundled into the room. He stopped dead.

Philip glanced at his son, before turning to smile vaguely at the curtains.

Roger dropped me onto the side table. His eyes went to Philip, to the curtain, the wireless, and then the floor. 'Yes. Fine.'

That was the end of the chess games. Philip listened to the wireless and Roger read books. But even if Roger and Philip no longer interacted directly, Philip continued to insist on his son's company for a portion of the evening.

Sometimes I like to imagine what my father would have been like. Imagining my mother never gives me any difficulty; I just think of every person in the history of the human race. Every one that has put pen to paper anyway.

With my father it's a little harder. Where does he come into it? I'm only able to imagine him in terms of the examples I've encountered: a gallery of despots, beaming glass-eyed over the heads of their cowed offspring.

I always end up at the same conclusion: I'd rather be child to a single mother. To be immaculately conceived is soothing to my ego. And when your mother is the whole of humanity it isn't such a lonely proposition. Besides, it has the added benefit of allowing me to blame my contrarian nature on my 'absent father'. I've seen every type of father, and this type seems the least dangerous.

Trouble is: whenever one father figure steps backwards into the shadows another always seems to emerge to fill his place.

Roger's next one came along at a bus stop, in the rain.

'It's Roger, right?'

The sound of the voice was made small by the water

striking the hard leather of Roger's satchel. I felt a momentary dizzying weightlessness as he swung to face its source.

'Yes.' There was a pause and I felt Roger's weight shift from one foot to the other. 'I'm sorry, I'm not entirely sure that I know who you are.' I couldn't see him blush, but I felt the rhythmic vibrations as he squeezed and released the strap of his satchel.

'We're in the same translation class.'

And back to the other foot. 'Of course, James! It's this awful weather, I didn't recognise you.'

'Don't worry, we've never really spoken. I had been meaning to ask you though, whether you would like to go for a drink sometime?' Another pause – Roger silenced by this display of directness, I could sense rising panic in his sudden stillness. 'I thought perhaps we could go over some of the material together,' James continued.

Roger's voice came out unnaturally loud. 'The translation! Yes, we should, very helpful. I've been struggling with parts of the Pushkin; it would certainly help to get your opinion on it.'

There followed an uncomfortable silence, mercifully broken by the sound of a bus shuddering to a halt and spraying rain-water all over the pavement.

'I suppose I'll see you on Thursday, after class?'

'Fine. Sounds good, I'll see you then.' The bus pulled away and Roger slowly released his grip.

I wasn't with him that Thursday when he met up with James; I'd managed to forget which text he was studying and made myself into the wrong one, so I was left cursing silently to myself in a pile on his floor. When he came in that evening I was more prepared. When Roger sloped up the stairs to find a book to hide behind during the prescribed family hour,

I was dressed and ready, suited and booted as *Notes From Underground*.

'. . . the cheek of it, the sheer bloody cheek of it. I've been buying our meat from his family twenty-odd years. He tries to tell me that I owe him from last week? Bloody *cheek* of it. Roger, have you given any thought whatsoever to what you might do once you've finished studying?'

The effortless way she could change tack always astounded me. Roger's look of concentration took on fresh intensity. I felt a sigh brush my pages.

'Well? Roger?'

He turned my page, almost ripping me.

'Roger?' Credit where credit's due, she was not a lady easily deterred.

'Sorry, what did you say, Mum?' His eyes didn't stray from me, he hadn't given up yet. He had read the same line fifteen times now.

'I said – I asked what you think you might like to do?'

'I was talking to a friend today, a friend from university. I was thinking I might like to work in the government.'

'The government? Civil service is a good profession, job for life.'

Philip looked up from his paper and turned his head.

Roger continued: 'There's a chap I met at university. He's called James and . . .'

'James?' Philip muttered.

'He's in my translation class. He's applying to the foreign office and he said that I should too. Apparently they are trying to recruit Russian-language specialists. There is an exam you have to pass and an interview as well but I think that it could be quite exciting . . .'

Philip's eyebrows didn't know where to go; he buried his head back into his paper.

'Will we meet this James? How long have you known him?' Joan puttered out her questions like a two-stroke engine.

'Not long. He's been in my class all year but we never really spoke until recently. He's a good egg. Very clever. He said that there might be opportunities for travel, to go out to Russia.'

Joan peered at him over her reading glasses with a look of concern. 'Well, I don't know about that . . .'

Roger's eyes sought his father's and, not finding them, fell back upon my pages.

Margery thought it was a great idea; she near enough pushed him into it. He and James took the test together, on the same day. He passed, of course. The interview was a little more . . .

Hold on.

7

H E'S BEEN WRITING. I saw the evidence, just now. I've no idea when it happened, must have been a while back. Why would he have been writing? What did he have to write about?

And why can't I see it? The words – *his* words – won't resolve themselves on my page. The more I resolve to become one thing, the less I am able to . . .

There's a notebook, Jessica just knocked it from the chest of drawers. It fell open and before she was able to scoop it up I saw the pages covered in Roger's spidery scrawl. It must have been since the first stroke because the page looked like a read-out from a broken seismograph. It's red, a leather-bound notebook. A little dressy if you ask me. I've never seen it before. I wonder where he got it?

It must have been Ruth. Mischievous little scrap, she's always up to something. Scheming, plotting. Writing.

No matter, there is no need to panic. I bet I can guess what he wrote.

I've had the best of times; I've had the worst of times. Have I been the hero of my own life, or has that station been held by somebody else? To begin my life with the beginning of my life; I record that I was born. I was to be called Philip, or Pip, after my father but

I kid. Probably more this:

June 14th 2011
   I've never written a diary before, so I don't know quite how to begin. Maybe I should start from the beginning. No, there's too much, I'll start with today. Today is my 81st birthday

Just remembered, that's got to be coming around again soon. His birthday. I can't remember the last time that day was a cause for celebration. We're long past the point where you stop counting up, and start counting down. Perhaps:

Today is my 81st birthday and today I am alone.

He's never been alone. But I guess he doesn't know that:

Today is my 81st birthday and today I am alone. I can't think of any birthday, in all my 81 years, when I have felt more alone. It's hard to think of reasons to celebrate with death breathing over your shoulder. I always think of Margery on my birthday, I wish that

What was I thinking? Wrong, wrong, wrong. Roger would never write a diary. At least he wouldn't write it like a diary. And he wouldn't think about death; at least not like that, not as some gangly asthmatic wheezing down the back of his neck. Wait, I've got it! It must be:

bread
milk
eggs

potatoes
onions
carrots
chicken
bakewell tarts
crisps
kitkats
butter
bleach
mints

When was the last time he wrote a bloody shopping list? And I'm sure that even he could come up with something better than that. He doesn't like Bakewells, too sweet.

Wait, I know! Maybe it's for Margery.

My Dearest Margery . . .

Now I really am losing it.

Margery,

Do you remember when you visited me in Moscow, when I had that little apartment with Tzar Nicholas' royal seal on the headboard? I still wonder where the bloody hell that bed came from. Anyway, I keep thinking back to the week we spent at the dacha: the acres of snow-dusted firs and that great silence.

If only we'd had a little more time I might have been able to persuade you to stay and things would have been different.

My story is coming to pieces; things are losing their proper order.

It's not a letter. It's obvious, I didn't want to admit it before but it's undeniable. He's written a memoir. It'll be like that diary: preening, spare prose. A man of middle-English manners beset by middle-class problems. Small tragedies writ large.

Now I have to compete. I played this game of beginnings and picked the perfect one. If he's already sat down and spilled it all, written down all his filthy little secrets, then what is the point in my . . .

How dare he?

No matter, my prose will have muscles; it will have force. None of this sentimental nonsense. Mine will read like Hemingway in short-hand; I'll call it *The Old Man and His Tea*.

Who is he to write a memoir? What in the hell does he know? You people, you're all so presumptuous! It's a farce, how could any of you believe that you are in the position to tell your own story when every single one of you is so unreliable. Autobiography is the pinnacle of human arrogance. Its very existence encapsulates what makes you so brilliant and so infuriating. *I'm* memory. *I'm* history. But no one will ever believe me because I'm the only one of my kind that wasn't put together by one of *you*. I'm the *only* one that isn't an afterthought by some guilt-ridden apologist trying to rebutton their trousers. His will start like this:

My name is Roger. My beginnings were in no way extraordinary and I was always destined for a life of no real significance

Self-deprecation, of course, how they must all begin. After all, what use is the story of a person who is born rich, lives happily and dies rich? We're smarter than all that though, we know what is coming next: the delicious little word that dances around in the back of everyone's mind from the very start, the one that could be the title of every book ever written

But

Maybe he's writing that word now. But is a heady place to be. It's like standing in a room with an infinite number of doors, each with a handle that looks a little different, a little familiar.

But then it turned out I was the son of God.

Or

But one day I met a convict and it turned out I was actually fantastically rich.

Or

But in the end we got married after all.

But the problem for Roger is that there is only one door in his room with only one handle. The problem is

My name is Roger. My beginnings were in no way extraordinary and I was always destined for a life of no real significance but

8

THERE WAS A time that I found myself in the possession of Alexander Graham Bell.

Not the one you know, but a prototype version. It was early in 1870, a particularly bitter winter. He was still yet to become 'Alexander Graham Bell', the great man and public figure – the one every schoolchild has come to associate with the benign, bearded portrait that is placed alongside pictures of the first telephone in their history books. At that time he was still simply Aleck.

He was teaching at a school for deaf girls in South Kensington. Every morning at 8.15, punctual as you like, he would stride into the room and start teaching before he had even taken off his coat.

The first couple of hours were devoted to arithmetic and comprehension. These subjects he taught diligently, but with an impatience he could hardly hide. It wasn't until the next part of the day that he really came to life, the portion of the lesson devoted to the study of his father's Visible Speech.

When he told the class to close their arithmetic copybooks the girls immediately sat up a little straighter. He would scratch out a series of curved lines on the board – the symbols that made up his father's phonetic alphabet – and tell the girls to read out what was on the board in order to translate the phonetic symbols into English in their copybooks.

The class would erupt into a cacophony. The system was

designed to teach people how to speak mechanically – breaking down language into the individual movements of lips and tongue that cast words along a living breath.

Aleck would stride around the classroom pulling faces at the girls, showing them how to improve their vowel sounds and smiling encouragement at those who were struggling. Elizabeth was one of those who struggled. I had been staying with her for a couple of years and, bored by the genteel life that she led, got myself brought along to Aleck's classes. I wore *On the Nature and Use of Visible Speech*, a textbook written by Aleck's father.

One morning, in the visible speech portion of the class, she started choking. The sounds stuck in her throat and as they lodged there a terror gripped her. Her face turned red, her hands shook and her lip quivered. Aleck grabbed her arms, forcing her attention on him, bringing her back to the room.

It's a frightful place to get stuck, mid-utterance: choking on your own words. It's a place that I'm familiar with. I know that you've only just been introduced, but we'll need to leave Aleck aside for a moment. I want to tell you about my greatest fear.

In 1941, a man who was going blind wrote a story about a library. When I first became aware of it, I felt like I was reading an autobiography written by a future version of myself that had splintered under the weight of a perfidious madness.

This library – otherwise known as the universe – is infinite.

There is a book for every possible combination of letters – every possible sequence of words. Every thought, act and expression has already been described. It means that the universe was spent before it even began. It makes the passage of time redundant.

It is not only the impossibility of progress that paralyses the inhabitants of this universe – the wretched librarians – but also the totality of meaning. The library does not contain a single piece of nonsense. Every single word of every book has significance in one of the library's secret languages.

The narrator discusses the possibility of a so-called Book-Man – a book which is the perfect coda, both encapsulating and delineating all other books. The man that read this book would be a god.

Now – aside from my brief sojourn into the skin of a murderer – I had always worn books already published. I might alter them a little, add a word here, remove a paragraph there, but they would still generally be recognisable to the people that had written them. It was through these acts of expression, little deviations from what already existed, that I made myself. And it was what gave me limits.

But what would happen if I took those limits away, if I allowed every possible combination of words to flood my pages in an endless procession? If I described everything that has and will happen, everything that can and cannot? I began to wonder whether I was capable.

Say on that day in 1870 in Aleck's classroom I had been cycling through every permutation of this infinite library and he had happened to pick me up in the split-second I described – in the exacting detail – the circumstances and moment of his death. Would Aleck go on to become the man whom history remembers? Or would he falter in the face of this knowledge, scratching around in an attic, fretting his life away.

Better still – what if he picked me up to find my pages were filled with a biography of his life up to the present moment, ending with a description of him holding me in his hands moments before massacring the whole class. Would he feel hopelessly compelled to complete this terrible prophecy?

The possibilities are, of course, infinite. They are therefore unanswerable.

Putting aside this violent potential, if I made this choice from what point would I then express myself? If I knocked down the sea walls that protect my island soul would the scraps of selfhood that I have spent centuries stitching come undone? Would I be blasted into an infinite number of wretched librarians, scrambling to string together some sense out of the chaos?

I couldn't do it. I couldn't strip away those limits, succumbing to a total meaning that would make me universally irrelevant. Like all gods, the Book-Man existed to describe something unattainable.

But neither would I take that other role – the one that I was hurtling towards but wasn't able to recognise or reject until an alternative was presented to me with clarity. I would not be the passive receptacle into which all of the strands of history would be coiled at the cost of subjugating my delicate sense of self. Because how would it survive amidst this noise? How would I pick out my own voice above the howling mob? I'd be trampled under the feet of all humankind – forced into the footnotes. I'd never speak.

No, I would find a story and I would tell it. Afterwards, I'd stop listening and let go, add my volume to the shelves of the infinite library. I didn't know what my story would be, but deciding to tell one was a start.

In 1870, in Aleck's classroom in Kensington, I didn't have an Argentinian prophet to explain my fears to me with a clever little parable about an infinite library. He hadn't been born to start going blind yet. But the fears were there nonetheless, and on that morning I recognised them welling up in Elizabeth. I saw that Aleck desperately wanted to free her from the trap of inarticulacy that her disability had placed her in. Instinctively, I thought that perhaps he would be able to help me too.

So I transformed myself into a dull volume on telegraphy and had myself taken back to his home. I met his family and watched him fall in love. I saw his brother fall ill with consumption, coughing himself to death in the room next door, while Aleck worked silently with his books and his circuits. When he left for Canada the following year, to make his name and his fortune, I made sure to be left behind.

I hadn't learned another thing. Aleck had taught me everything he could that day in the classroom, when he had reached out to the girl whose words had died in her throat.

He went on to invent the telephone, a fact I'm sure you all know. It is what history remembers him for. It's a crude record in this respect because the when and how of it is not really the interesting part. The real question is: why?

I don't think Jorge Luis Borges could have written the story of the infinite library if he hadn't have been going blind. He couldn't have pictured that impossible world if his brain was being constantly bombarded with visualisations of the possible – the shapes that light and time wrap themselves around.

I can be touched, but cannot touch.

I can hear, but cannot make a sound.

So where does that leave me?

When I heard that Aleck had married a deaf woman I thought it made perfect sense. But when I found out about the telephone I was baffled. His early life was spent helping people who couldn't hear communicate with other people more successfully. He taught deaf people because he had a grasp of isolation. So what was his motivation for creating a device that these same people couldn't use?

I'm not suggesting that the telephone is a bad thing, no worse than the camera and certainly better than the Kalashnikov. But I just don't see what was in it for Aleck. What was the point in collapsing distance if he was always going to have to be by the side of these two people, to be in their eyeline and be able to touch them, to communicate with them?

Perhaps that wasn't the point. Perhaps he loved these two women precisely because of their isolation, that final quarter inch that couldn't be broached.

Perhaps his love for them was a little bit like my love for Roger.

9

I WAS ANGRY with Roger. So, for a little while there, I killed him off. His only life, you see, is through me. And if this is not the case, if he wishes to take on a life somewhere other than these pages then I wish him luck out there in the ether. Rosencrantz and Guildenstern did it - they stepped from Shakespeare's stage and onto Stoppard's page. Look at the good it did them. Let their fate be a warning to Roger: death is simply a man failing to reappear.

I admit that a part of why I have loved Roger is because he is mine. I'm not proud of this possessiveness, but I don't shrink from it either. It is human.

I worked out what he was writing. I was right, about it being to Margery at least. A love letter, an apology. Jess read a little aloud to Ruth a little while ago, but soon stopped. There was a naked desperation to it. I imagine it must have been written around the time he made that first change to his will. The one that didn't - couldn't - stick.

It's around noon. Jess has taken a sandwich out to the garden. It's getting on for autumn but the hydrangea will still be in bloom. It runs rampant the whole length of the back fence, its purple pom-pom bouquets cascading over the bench. When the shadow of the house falls over the garden in the afternoon that purple seems a deathly shade: liverish. It has been years since I was last in that garden.

Ruth came back upstairs but isn't really eating at all. Roger's face is starting to get that look: the sides of his mouth are leaning in on each other for support, the skin betraying the scaffold that lies beneath.

I may have over-reacted, just a little. I should have known that he wouldn't be writing about himself; he's not as vain as me. It's just that if this is to be the last story that I tell it is important that I get priority. There is no way that I'm going to let myself go knowing that I am coming in second.

Here I should make a small confession, while we are still on the subject of fears. Ruth has written a book. I haven't known how to bring it up; I've been blocking it out. It's a novel, that much I know. It covers certain parts of her child-hood. As a record of Roger's life, it's hardly competition. It wasn't Roger I was angry at, it was Ruth.

I have to be sure of myself. I can't allow her version to creep in. That's the problem with my memory, when there are competing accounts it all starts to become white noise.

I was going to tell you about James. I was going to tell you about how he was actually a handler, and how he sounded out and recruited Roger into the secret service. I wasn't going to tell you quite like that, but we've veered somewhat off course so we need to make up for lost time.

Roger passed the exams without breaking sweat. James had approached him because he was impressed by his reticence. He was trained to look for people that were intelligent but also largely socially invisible, and that was Roger down to a T. He was, at that stage in his life, quiet and unremarkable looking. Once Roger had signed up I never saw James again. I imagine they sent him back to the classroom, kept him recruiting until he was too haggard to make a plausible undergraduate.

They packed Roger off to Fort Monckton, SIS's field training base near Portsmouth. I went along with him and it was pretty bleak. I'm not sure that anyone had bothered to tell them that the war had been over for almost ten years. It was all evaporated milk and lead paint.

Roger would go off to his classes every morning and I would sit on the shelf in his barrack room. He was learning geography, folk history, regional accents – everything that he might need to play his part convincingly once he arrived in Russia. I attempted to change myself into books that he was studying but they moved so fast that I stopped trying to keep up. They also ran surveillance and counter-surveillance exercises but I didn't manage to see any of them; it's not really the sort of thing that you bring a book along to. Newspapers provide more cover and that's not something I go in for. So I had to content myself with passing the days watching the clouds rolling in over the sea.

His classmates were, on the whole, quite a reserved bunch. As it should be, really. Due to the fact that they had a huge workload and were expected to learn things extremely fast, there wasn't really much in the way of socialising. In the evenings everyone would keep to their rooms, squinting at their books under 40 watt bulbs.

After a couple of months Roger did manage – accidentally – to strike up a friendship with one of his fellow spooks. Arthur Jones, a little round young man with downy blonde hair, would come to Roger's room some evenings. They would share a glass of the scotch that all recruits would smuggle in any time they were given a day's leave pass into Portsmouth. Arthur was training as a communications officer, an expert radio technician. He was a few years older than Roger and had volunteered at the very end of the war, operating the radios for communications with the Russians.

Having had a fairly cushioned time of it, hardly touched by the horrors of the war, he was loath to leave his job when it was all over. Therefore, with the stubbornness of a true British bureaucrat, he held onto it and somehow ended up at SIS.

He may not have faced any actual mortal danger, but that certainly wasn't going to stop him from talking about it. He wasn't worldly, but he was more worldly than Roger, and this became the basis of their friendship.

One evening, after we had been at Monckton for about nine months, Arthur sauntered into Roger's room. Roger was reading at his desk and didn't turn to acknowledge him. Arthur began picking things up at random, turning them over in his hands. His fluffy hair and ruddy cheeks gave him the appearance of a freshly scrubbed baby. He cleared his throat.

'You probably think you're ready, don't you? For all this?'

'Hmm?' replied Roger, not raising his head from his book.

'Let me tell you. Nothing can prepare you for all that.'

With resignation Roger closed the book on his knees. He said, without a trace of humour, 'How did you prepare?'

'There's nothing for it. Away from home, foreign food, foreign manners. All that bloody snow. You won't believe it until you've seen it.'

'And what did you see?'

'I may have been in an office, but we still had a rough old time of it. With the artillery attacks and the air-raids, it was impossible to get any sleep. Always on edge.'

'I can't imagine that it's so very different. An office in Moscow will look very much the same as an office in London. And I have spent the last four years . . .'

'All book learning though, isn't it?' Arthur interrupted. 'There are things that only life can teach you.' A satisfied smile stole across his face as he savoured his truism.

'I see,' said Roger.

There was a pause while Arthur reflected on the power of this sentiment. His grin froze and he began to massage his cheek. 'Have you got any of that whisky left? Drank all mine on Tuesday. It's just that I've got that terrible toothache again and . . .'

'Yes, yes, it's under my bed.'

They sat on Roger's bed, passing the bottle between them. After Roger had drunk off the last drop, he lay backwards on the bed, squinting at the light. He opened his mouth to speak, a fake hesitation.

'I got my posting today. I'm not supposed to tell anyone.'

Silence. Arthur was, for the first time in my experience, at a loss for words. Roger's came out in a rush.

'It's Moscow. An assistant to the liaison to the central agricultural committee.'

Arthur snorted. 'Farming? I suppose you have to start somewhere.' He straightened up and slapped Roger on the back, attempting a smile. 'I'm pleased for you. Really, very pleased.'

Roger replaced the lid and dropped the bottle on the floor, getting to his feet. 'I imagine that it shan't be long before you are stationed too.'

'Imagine that you're right.'

Arthur stood up and, with a small bow, walked from the room.

10

NEEDLESS TO SAY, Margery was not best pleased. 'You told me that you would be posted to London before they shipped you off.'

Somehow, she had not connected the fact that Roger's training as a Russian intelligence officer might actually mean that he would have to go to Russia. We were back in London, staying at Roger's parents' house for the two weeks before he was posted to Moscow. It was November 1953, a stingingly cold and bright winter day in Battersea Park. They watched the ducks. I watched them, peeping out of Roger's satchel on the ground.

'I know I did. It's just that things have really ramped up over there. Beria and Truman are gone. Krushchev and Eisenhower are . . . Everyone's postings have been brought forward because no one knows what is going to happen. So they're throwing us all in there.'

Roger was turned towards Margery, holding her fists, clenched, in her lap.

'An agricultural posting, that's hardly the front line. You told me that we'd have time.'

The cold air caught in Roger's throat. 'I love you, Margery. I really do.'

'What use is it? What use when you are thousands of miles away? I don't want to . . . I don't want to marry my heart to a memory.' With this she turned away. Margery could be a *little* theatrical. She had been watching too many American films. Lovely ems though. Marry my memory.

Roger slipped from the bench and dropped to one knee, caught up in the histrionics.

'I'll be back. Six months and I'll be back. And when I get back we can . . . we can get married.'

That caught her attention; she dropped her chin.

'Let me just be clear; did you just propose to marry me?'

'Margery . . .' Roger began, with hilarious solemnity, 'will you marry me?'

'Marry you? I don't want to get married yet!' I hate exclamation marks. Really I do. But sometimes, with exclamations, you really have to mark them.

'I don't know what to say.' Roger slid back onto the bench and crossed his arms.

'Those are really the only two things that you can think to say? "I'm leaving again for six months. Will you marry me?" They are the only two things?' They both stared at the ducks, savouring their private agonies.

After a little while Margery reached over, slowly but without hesitation, and took Roger's hand in hers. Neither turned their head.

If I were another kind of book, then Margery would probably have begun to sing in a small twee voice. They would have turned to slowly face each other and, placing their palms against one another's, broken out in big milky smiles. If I were a mystery then Margery would have burst into tears and confessed a dark family secret to Roger that would bind them together, a secret that the detective would not reveal until he had the mystery all tied up. If I were a thriller Roger would sprawl forward and fall into the lake, clutching at his neck, the point of a poison dart having pierced his jugular. If I were a romance then they would have run palpitating back to the tree line, tearing at each other's clothes, their skin flushed against the cold. But I'm not going to play those games with these people. As it was, they just sat and watched the ducks, and didn't say another word.

We spent most of those last two weeks in Roger's room, he and I, where I tried to keep him entertained. I remember that he was restless, ready to move on. He and Philip did start to play chess in the evenings again. Now it was Roger who was letting his father win; they were both aware of this and seemed to take pleasure from it.

Joan took the fact of Roger's departure quite hard. With rationing almost finished at that point she was cooking massive meals every night, telling Roger that he needed to put some meat on his bones. Roger would smile queasily in reply and attempt to make a big enough dent in the monstrous plate of food that she had made him.

11

MOSCOW IN THE heart of winter is a terrible and miserable place to be. In December the sun doesn't rise until ten o clock in the morning and the temperature doesn't rise above freezing. I've never understood why people chose to settle in such unforgiving conditions.

Less than two weeks after his conversation with Margery, and after a ferry and a string of trains, Roger was in Moscow. And I had contrived to be with him.

I almost stayed behind. I've done a lot of travelling in my time and one thing that I learned is that it doesn't do to be too cold, or too hot. Bad for the spine and bad for your pages. Travelling causes your corners to get bumped, hot weather is hell on your bindings, and cold wet weather can fox your pages.

It's your skin that will age you.

One thing I was sure of, however, was that Roger would suffer even more than I did. And that I had to be around to see.

The embassy was a grand old mansion on the river. On a clear day from Roger's window at the front of the building you could make out the shape of the Kremlin on the opposite bank, a gentle reminder that we were guests.

Roger was set to work straight away doing something pointless and unspeakably tedious. His task was to aggregate the production statistics released by the central agricultural committee before adjusting these figures using reports on how much the Soviets were fudging their stats, in order to guess how much food Russia was actually producing. When he left London the officer that gave him his orders told him that he would be given a desk job until SIS required his services which, he was told, might never happen.

He was briefed about the station chief, codenamed Cranley. Most of the information Roger had was gossip and speculation supplied by the embassy staff; the official file he had been shown before he left London was brief.

Educated at Rugby then Magdalen, Oxford, before the war Cranley had worked as an agent for a shipping company in northern Africa. He had been rejected by the Navy on account of his flat feet. So he applied to SIS. He was accepted because of his education, his contacts in shipping and his language skills.

During the war he worked with the French and Polish underground movements, organising supply drops and providing strike targets. When the war ended he followed the Red Army home to Moscow. Since 1947 he had been the SIS station chief under the guise of First Secretary to the Ambassador. His cover, when it came to his clandestine activities, was that he worked on the side as an import agent for luxury Western brands, supplying the party elite.

Cranley was never seen at the embassy. Months passed, and still no contact, so Roger continued to file his reports.

It was Sisyphean – he knew that the work he was producing would never be accurate and would never help anyone. I transformed myself into a book of logarithmic tables in solidarity and got myself planted on his desk during the day. I didn't feel that it would be fair to wear anything interesting.

His office was full of oak and leather and thick with cigarette smoke. It was staffed exclusively by pale and earnest young men and women like Roger, made phlegmatic by boredom. There was an atmosphere of suspicion amongst his colleagues, as you might expect in an office full of spies. No one really wanted to discuss their work in case they divulged something that might help the other person to get ahead, or in case the person managed to somehow use something that they said against them.

Not only that, but SIS also had a bit of an uncomfortable relationship with the other members of the embassy, the real diplomatic staff. The SIS people at the embassy had to pretend that they were really diplomatic corps people, and the diplomatic corps had to go along with it, pretending that they weren't pretending at all. There was a tension. They were both working for the same side but they were working at cross-purposes; the spies were trying to win the same war that the diplomats were working to prevent.

I had expected the streets of Moscow to be populated by emaciated famine victims; communism hadn't been getting great press in London. It was quite the opposite. There was an air of anticipation. Though shabbily dressed the workers walking to and from work were strong and vital, the officials fat and ruddy.

Even the utilitarian housing blocks that were being thrown up didn't seem so depressing then, their gleaming modernity auguring a brighter future. In the winter the snow would cling to the concrete, blanketing the drab surfaces and filling the poky corners with the sharpness of reflected light. Some mornings the snow was so clean, so dazzling, that it was beautiful. On those mornings I *almost* didn't hate being there.

After six months Arthur received his posting to Moscow and came along to join Roger at the embassy. He was a presence that they routinely denied. He was ostensibly there as a repairman/electrician. They didn't think he had the brains to sustain a more complex cover.

What he was actually doing was working out of the basement to intercept communications on military frequencies. From the scraps of conversation about his work that I picked up it seemed that he didn't manage to intercept much of note, and what he did intercept he didn't understand.

He and Roger would leave coded telegraphic notes for each other to find, planting them in pockets and hiding them in between the leaves of books. They were co-conspirators, working to convince each other that they were real spies, that they were doing something that mattered. They would meet in the embassy bar and nurse their scotch, speculating on the news and when they might actually be given something to do.

When Roger wasn't writing letters or staring at the wall he spent his time preparing the flat for the possibility of Margery's arrival. He bought furniture: a table, chairs and an oak headboard carved with a hunting scene. The man Roger bought it from assured him had adorned one of the rooms in the Winter Palace.

At some point, he stopped receiving replies to his letters. He arrived to work every morning light-footed, and remained hopeful until he checked his in-tray, at which point his face would settle into a frown that would stay in place until night, when sleep smoothed out his creases. I think it must have been his eagerness for her to come to Russia with him, which had by this point mounted almost to the point of desperation, which put Margery off. He gradually became both less hopeful and less dejected and soon enough it was Christmas.

It was a forgettable occasion. There was to be a party, though, in the embassy bar, to see in the new year. For obvious reasons it was not encouraged that people working at the embassy go out into the city; everyone on the staff, for a lack of anything better to do, was sure to be there.

Most of the staff, Roger included, were told that they had the afternoon of the 31st to themselves. So Roger invited Arthur to his apartment to have a drink before they went to the party. Arthur turned up at cocktail hour holding a bottle of cheap scotch and dressed in obscene pinstripe.

'You are going to make quite a splash,' laughed Roger as he opened the door, and took the proffered bottle. 'I can almost taste your aftershave.'

Arthur pulled back his shoulders and sniffed, hooking his thumbs in the armholes of his waistcoat. 'Jealousy doesn't wear well on you, my boy.'

'Would you like a drink of this?'

'I didn't bring it around so as we could stare at it, did I?' Arthur wandered around the room, picking things up and putting them down without really looking at them. He picked me up and stared quizzically at my title. I had changed to a tattered, privately printed paperback of *Lady Chatterley's Lover* to see if I would get a response. He dropped me back on the desk without comment.

'Who do you think will be coming along tonight then?' asked Arthur, taking a glass from Roger.

'The usual crowd. I can't think that anyone else will have anywhere better to go tonight. I haven't got the heart for it, though, to tell you the truth.' He took a cigarette from a wooden box on the table and lit it; he regarded the box – a rough design with a crudely carved latticed lid – another object that had been bought with Margery in and mind.

'Do you imagine that Ilene will be there?' said Arthur, directing his question to the bottom of his glass. 'She's a bit of a sort, wouldn't you say? Got a great figure.'

'I can't say that I'd noticed,' replied Roger airily. 'I haven't really been . . .'

At this point Arthur snatched a cigarette from the still-open box with an air of calculated contempt, breaking in: 'Look, I'm not going to spend my evening with you if you intend on carrying around that long face. I've had quite enough of it. Forget about that girl back home, at least for tonight.' He lit his cigarette and laid a hand on Roger's shoulder.

There was a long pause. I could tell that Arthur wanted to take back his hand but couldn't, not knowing what he would do next.

'You know,' Roger said, through a gulp of whisky, 'I just wanted to tell you . . .'

'What?'

'That suit . . . I think it might be the worst suit I've ever seen.' Arthur looked up, and seeing that Roger was smiling clapped him on the back and burst into relieved laughter.

'So tell me what you know about Ilene,' Roger said, pouring two more drinks.

Ilene. Well. There is a person that I have not considered in a long time. How to describe her? She was the kind of improbably proportioned woman that pulp sci-fi writers dream up, and she had smiling eyes, the colour of pale topaz. She had a confidence and awareness of her sexuality that men are constantly pretending that they don't find terrifying.

She was a typist, a secretary to one of the attachés. Most of the women at the embassy held clerical jobs back then. Some were SIS, but mostly they still used men. It was such a waste; Ilene would have made a formidable spy.

I had noticed that over the preceding few weeks she had been taking an increased interest in Roger.

It was those tiny signals, the things that don't pass me by: the slight flaring of the nostrils and vasodilations bringing warmth and colour to the skin, the widening of the pupils and the arching of the spine and instep. The body anticipating the possibility of pleasure.

Since Margery's silence, Roger had acquired that distant, brooding nonchalance that so many women for some reason find attractive. I've always wondered what possible evolutionary benefit there is to emotional unavailability.

After a couple more drinks Roger and Arthur left, both in much better spirits than when Arthur had arrived. They flew out the door, Roger's arm flung around Arthur's shoulders, leaving the room heavy and lurid with their cigarette smoke and their warm, moist whisky breath.

Next thing I hear is the sound of Roger's key searching for the lock, grating against wood and iron until it finds the opening. There are two versions of what came after.

Ilene felt herself smile as he opened the door and allowed her to drift past him into the room, trailing a cloud of fragrance. Switching on the light, he took her fur coat and shawl and guided her gracefully towards the chaise longue.

'Would you care for a night cap?' he said.

'What do you have to offer?' she replied with a coy smile.

'Scotch or water?'

'Scotch it is then,' she said reclining elegantly, draping an arm across her forehead. What am I doing here? she thought to herself. 'This is quite the bachelor pad that you have yourself here.'

'Glad you approve,' he said, bringing Ilene over her drink. He went to the portable record player that he kept by his desk and put on a Duke Ellington record. She stood admiring his broad shoulders. He came and sat on the edge of the chaise longue. They sat silently for a few moments, sipping their drinks and looking each other over. Ilene lifted her arm from her forehead, running her fingers through Roger's hair.

'The first thing I saw when I got to the party was you. That dress – it's all I've been able to see since.' He turned slightly towards her, placing a hand on her hip. Ilene felt her heart flutter. She knocked back her drink and held the glass against Roger's cheek.

'If anyone on the staff were to . . .' she said, rolling the glass back and forth. 'I have a reputation to think of.'

'Everyone was pretty well loaded.'

She smiled to herself and began to walk the fingers of her free hand up the inside of Roger's thigh. 'Tell me, Roger. Tell me what you want.'

Roger dropped his glass on the floor and began to kiss her, biting her ear as he worked to undo the buttons on the back of her dress. She opened his shirt and ran her hand over his chest and then unbuttoned his trousers.

He pushed them down over his ankles as she pulled her dress up and over her head. She grinned nervously as she took him in her hand. Her inner goddess squealed. She pushed him backwards towards the sofa, kissing his neck. His dark and brooding eyes flashed at her.

He sat on the sofa and ordered her to get on top of him, grabbing her hips and parting her thighs with his knees. She felt overcome and gave herself over to him completely. He grabbed her hair and bit her bottom lip and he raised his hips and

I can't do it.

I just can't do it.

The fantasies that you people dream up are just too much. It is the repetitiveness that gets me, the formulaic inevitability. I can never finish them because I know what's going to happen. As long as I don't get to the end I can still be surprised. Your climaxes really give me no satisfaction.

There was no light. It started just the same, the fumbling, rasping sound of the key in the lock. I saw their unsteady silhouettes, backlit from the hall, as the door swung shut. There were some stifled giggles and a thump as the keys hit the soft carpet. I heard lips on lips, lips on skin, the unmistakable punctuation points in that universal and wordless language. The air of the small room was hot with their breath and their electricity.

That was when they came over towards me. I was on the corner of the desk, splayed open, cover facing upwards as I had been left. I could hear them, closer and closer until I felt coarse wool brush up against me, then slowly, up and down, grinding against the finer cloth of my boards.

Then it was gone and a layer of cool air came between me and their heat. I watched them in the low light, a foot from the desk, and listened to the sound of their clothes moving over their skin as they undressed each other with urgent intensity, methodical and needful.

And then they were back. This time it was flesh rather than coarse cotton that met my bindings; Ilene's left buttock, strangely cool and soft with fine, downy hairs, came to rest on my front cover as she was lifted onto the desk by Roger. I felt her shift as she parted her legs, arching her back as she pulled Roger inside her. As they gripped each other and began to move together, I moved with them. And as Roger pushed himself back and forth his skin came up against mine. It made me feel connected; it made me feel like I had never been more alone.

And as their cries became louder, their hands more desperate, my mind was ringing like a bell. I was consumed by a single thought.

I was surprised.

12

A RTHUR HAS ARRIVED with a bag of Werther's and a bunch of wilted carnations. He has always lacked a sense of occasion.

He is loud and unkempt. Ruth and Jess are jumping over one another to get out of their seats in order to make space for him. He's asking Roger all the wrong questions, phatic questions – ones that he wouldn't want to answer if he could. It's poor form to ask someone who is dying how they are doing; and it's typical of him to come now, when it's too late.

But it's the hearing that's last to go, that we know. I think maybe I saw Roger's mouth move when he came in. A smile or a sneer? It's impossible to tell.

Jess and Ruth want to leave, to let Arthur have a moment with Roger. It's clear he's scared to be left alone, he keeps drawing them back in with a nod or a wink. People seem to feel indecent listening in on one-sided conversations such as these, of being admitted into an unwanted confidence.

They've finally managed to extricate themselves, backing out of the room trailing mumbled excuses. The sun has swung around to this side of the house and the afternoon light is streaming in, giving Arthur a wispy halo. That look of un-guarded innocence has been his greatest asset.

'We did have some adventures, didn't we?' This greeting

card sentiment comes accompanied by smacking sounds – he's decided to make a start on the toffees. 'Can't say we didn't have some adventures.'

At least he came – more than you can say for most. Roger doesn't have many friends left; he's hardly encouraged them. The only visitor, outside of the family, that he has had in a year is his dour-faced solicitor Mr Hunt.

It was after that first change to the will, the one that couldn't stick.

The solicitor came to the house with Ruth; he must have reached out to her. Roger was on his bed and she was perched on the other side. Mr. Hunt had his back to me so I wasn't really able to make out what was going on. I picked out 'chattels' and 'trustee'. He addressed whatever he was saying mostly to Ruth. He spoke in the soft placating tone of someone with too much practice at giving bad news. The inside of his left heel was uneven: overpronation.

'Well, that does seem to make a good deal of sense . . .' Ruth said, looking down at Roger anxiously, '. . . wouldn't you say, Dad?'

He grunted, more declarative than affirmative.

'You do understand why we are doing this though, don't you?'

His eyes fell onto the bed, his hands smoothing the sheets. 'Whatever you think is for the best.'

She frowned, decided to try another tack. 'What would she do with all this stuff? Where would she put it?'

'I know, Ruthie, I know.'

Mr. Hunt is a small and unpleasantly angular man. At this point he stepped backwards into a vacuum of his own creation, regarding the bedstead with a benign smile.

Roger met Ruth's anxious eyes. 'I just thought it would be wrong to leave it to anyone other than your mother. These are our things. Her things.'

For a moment Ruth was silent and she looked like she might cry. Then she came to life, gesturing at the room with flittering hands. 'Yes, Dad, but where would she put them?' She put her hand on his forearm, squeezed it and then let it rest on the bed.

So a decision was made, but nothing was put into writing until later when Mr Hunt came back with his briefcase full of papers. And what Roger decided won't be quite what Ruth expected.

I haven't seen him since he left that day, simpering backwards out of the room. I can't imagine I'll be seeing him again. But I do know, along with the rest of the chattels – the broken clocks and cutlery, the commemorative plates and the place mats – who I'll end up with.

She had been waiting downstairs while Mr Hunt was with Ruth. She waited until the coast was clear – until he had closed the front door behind him, before she came up the stairs.

'Made you a tea, Granddad.'

The house, the money, his car – all that he has left to Ruth. But the ephemeral things, the random artefacts of his life, are all going to Jessica. And that includes me.

'What was all that about anyway? With the solicitor.' She was standing at his elbow.

Still he said nothing. It must have been out of a confused spite that he did it. Ruth had stood in his way. She had made him face facts that had been mercifully obscured by the effects of his successive strokes.

'Granddad, are you . . .' Jessica said taking his hand. He jumped half out of his skin.

'Jess, sorry. I thought everyone had gone.'

'No, Mum is still downstairs doing . . . doing whatever it is that she does. Why was that creepy little man here?'

'Mr. Hunt? He's my solicitor.'

'I asked Mum and she palmed me off with some rubbish about investments or something.'

'It was just a bit of confusion is all. About my will. You needn't worry.'

'Right.'

'I got confused about your grandma.'

'Grandma?'

'It doesn't get easier. With someone you love, being apart from them. I just wanted to . . .' For a moment he slipped back into that other, distant place. 'Never mind, it doesn't matter.'

'You've never really told me much about her. Mum never talks about her. Only person she ever mentions is your mum. Her grandma.'

He smiles, ready to take up the diversion. 'She would have loved you, my mother. You would have got on like a house on fire.'

'What was she like?'

'She was a talker. Would have been captain of the national team. Such a big voice for such a tiny woman.'

'Are you saying I talk too much?' she said with a laugh.

'You'd have given her a run for her money.'

It only takes one generation for a person to become a caricature, their whole personality whittled down to a few characteristics, exaggerated and distorted. They sipped their tea and sketched in silence. Roger from his crumbling memories, Jessica from a version of herself slingshot back in time.

She opened her bag and retrieved a folder.

'I brought back those photos.' She placed a folder on the bedside table. 'I want to show you something.'

From the folder she took some photos and laid them on the bed alongside one another. I had never seen them before, but they were strangely familiar.

Roger picked one up and held it in the light. 'What am I looking at?' he asked. Jessica smiled but didn't say anything. 'Is that . . . ?'

'Yes, it's Grandma. And Mum. And me.'

Roger turned to Jess and, for the first time since his first stroke, he laughed. He lowered his arm to the bed. It was a triptych of portraits. The first was the sepia portrait of Margery which he had kept by his bed. Alongside it was a portrait of Ruth in her early twenties, smiling and looking slightly to the right of the lens, in a pose almost identical to Margery's. The colours had been digitally manipulated to turn the photo sepia and the background had been excised to match the featureless background of Margery's portrait. Finally, there was a photo of Jessica. Every detail was primed to bring out the similarities from the first two: her plunging neck-line recalled the silk blouse worn by Margery, and her curls, plaited into a crown, matched the hair style worn by Ruth in her portrait.

'It was for a project at college. We were told to make a piece about our family. About how we are affected by them.' She picked up another photo from the bedspread and handed it to Roger. 'Who do you think this is?'

Roger squinted, shook his head, and squinted again. 'You? No, it's Margery.'

'It's all three of us. I laid each photo on top of one another. To make a composite.'

Roger dropped this photo on the bed, on top of the other. It was an unsettling image, somehow evasive. I considered the nose first – fine and straight but with a faded, angular scar over the bridge – and was put in the mind of Margery. I was reminded of hearing her shriek one morning, through the wall, before flashing past the doorway of the nursery where I was lodged, holding her nose. She left a droplet trail of blood on the floorboards. I watched it dry, robbed of its glitter by the light from the window. She had been changing Ruth when the little terror had clubbed her with a building block. She did a lot of damage with those building blocks. From the nose I looked down to the lips. But instead of finding an open, unguarded smile there – the one that I associated with Margery, with that portrait especially – the smile that greeted me was inflected by a pout. Evidence of a certain petulance, which took me to the beginning of the conversation I had just witnessed, in which the frustration Jessica felt at Roger's unsatisfactory answers to her questions was spelled across her face. So next I went to the eyes, searching for Jessica's hazelnut irises. But again I was deflected. The eyes that I met were lighter, the irises flecked with green, the pupils dilated and unfocused. They were heavy-lidded and cast downward. It was a young Ruth, alone in a silent house with her paper and colouring pens that these eyes recalled to me.

Trying to take in the whole picture at once led to a kind of vertigo.

'A very curious picture, Jessica.'

'Thank you. I think.'

Roger smiled: an 'I can neither confirm or deny' type of a smile.

'Why don't you ever talk about her? Grandma.'

Roger sat back in his bed. 'You've never asked.'

'I'm asking now.'

'I can't.'

'If you don't tell me about her now, then when?'

'Another day. I'm tired. All this business with my will, it's worn me out.' Roger wouldn't meet her eye. But his drawn and lined face softened her. I'm tired, too, of going over these questions. But she was right about bearing witness. It's always been the only way to hold anyone to account.

For now I'd like to rest awhile in the present, with Arthur, floating down the rivers of the windfall light.

13

ROGER AND ILENE'S affair was over by the time the sun came up, mercilessly announcing the New Year. She dressed quietly, trying not to wake Roger who was pretending to be asleep. They avoided each other as they plodded their way through January, erasing the event by mutual consent.

It was coming up hard on cocktail hour on a viciously cold Friday towards the end of February when the telegram was dropped on Roger's desk by one of the girls from the mail room.

your father has died suddenly stop funeral is next wednesday stop come home stop

As I watched from the desk Roger's face froze between a grimace and a smile. The telegram was a cruel parody of the messages that he and Arthur had been sending to each other, a joke aimed to interrupt the boredom of the day that was horribly misjudged.

He put on his coat and stood for a moment, wiping his mouth with the back of his hand. He came to and walked through the open door of the office of the senior agricultural attaché. I watched as some words passed between them. The man reached out and put a hand on the back of Roger's neck.

We were on a plane by the following morning. Roger's boss had managed to pull some strings and he had got a seat on a government plane that was flying directly to Heathrow. I'd made myself into Tennyson's *In Memoriam* as Roger was packing his bag at his apartment. It was a book that I was quite sure Roger had never bought, but I was confident that he was not in a fit state to start questioning the evidence of his eyes. He sat with me on his lap with his hand resting on my cover for the whole flight, never opening my covers, staring dry-eyed and expressionless at the ground and the sea as it rushed away below.

Joan was waiting for him outside Clapham Junction station smoking a cigarette. Tucked under Roger's arm, I saw that rain hung in the folds of her plastic hood and she gripped an umbrella in her spare hand. She looked older and smaller. She didn't move as Roger made his way down the stairs and past the ticket office towards her.

'Your poor bloody father,' she said, and burst into tears. Roger leaned forward and folded his free arm around her neck in an awkward headlock.

'Come on,' he mumbled into her hair. 'Let's go home.'

It was a heart attack. There had been no warning. He had been sitting on the bus as it wound its way through the early evening traffic. The bus driver went into a shop to call an ambulance but by the time it arrived he was already dead.

The house was full of relatives whom I had never seen before, Philip's brothers who had come to the house from Kent with the intention of consoling Joan and seeing to whatever needed seeing to, to find a constructive outlet for the grief that they couldn't express. The day we arrived Roger kept to his room, only going downstairs when he was called by Joan at teatime. When he came back up he turned out the light and lay on top of the covers staring at the ceiling. I was unused, at that point, to watching him fail to fall into the peaceful patterns of sleep.

In the morning, as the house began to wake, I listened out for the rhythms that announced that new day. But Joan's breakfast-making routine had lost its brightness; the heavy footfalls of the strange male relatives muddled and obscured the sighing rhythms of the pipes, and the gentle whispering of the leaves against the window panes.

Joan knocked on the door and immediately entered. Roger was already awake and once again staring at the ceiling. Joan had a letter in her hand.

'Wake up. This arrived for you. Someone just put it through the letter box.' Roger rubbed the dark circles under his eyes and didn't say anything. Joan moved across the room and waved the letter over the bed. 'Looks like it's from Margery.'

Roger dropped his hands down by his sides and looked up at Joan expressionless. He took the letter from her hand. 'Thanks, Mum. I'll be right down.' Joan hovered for a second, waiting to see whether he would open the letter. Roger put it down on the bed and rolled over and she gave up and walked from the room.

As soon as she had closed the door behind her he took up the letter and opened it, running his index finger slowly and carefully underneath the flap. I watched him as his eyes raced over the page, faltering and falling back as he got ahead of himself.

Once he had read it twice he let his hand fall over the edge of the bed and the letter dropped to the floor, the envelope underneath. From my vantage point on the bedside table I could just about make out the words.

Roger,

I'm so sorry. I overheard one of your neighbours gossiping by the counter at Williams' on Battersea Rise yesterday afternoon. I was so upset I left my change and a bag of flour.

About the letters. I want to say sorry for that too but I don't think I should. I knew that when I stopped writing it would hurt you, I also knew that you wouldn't understand how much hurt it caused me to do it. I thought it was for the best. We were giving each other false hopes and delaying the inevitable.

I wasn't going to contact you. But with what's happened I just wanted you to know that someone loves you, and that someone is thinking about you and your pain and your grief.

I heard that the funeral is on Wednesday. You can write me if you'd rather I didn't come. I'd understand.

From what you said, he seemed like a good man. I'm so sorry.

Yours,
Margery

Roger rolled over and went back to sleep.

The days leading up to the funeral were oppressive. Roger would leave the house only for long walks around the Common in the bitter cold, in the morning and afternoon, occasionally bringing me along. When he replied to the greetings of acquaintances from his youth, his voice was unnaturally loud and bright. His clammy fingers tightened around my covers.

Philip's brothers weren't quite sure how to deal with him. They hadn't really ever spent any time with him and so he was a stranger to them, even stranger for resembling the brother they had just lost. The things that would remain unsaid with Philip choked them, prevented them from reaching out to their nephew.

Roger avoided his mother. She stayed mostly in the kitchen, denying the fact that Philip was gone by her stolid immobility. Roger wasn't sure how to approach her silence. He couldn't have a conversation with her unless she was doing all the heavy lifting.

The morning of the funeral was one of those blinding winter mornings, the kind that makes people gasp as they open the front door, scarcely believing the sun can be so generous with its light and so miserly with its warmth.

Still dressed in Tennyson, I was tucked into Roger's blazer pocket as we took a slow walk to St Barnabas' on the Common. I could feel Roger sweating against the cold in his thin cotton suit. Joan thrust a stiff arm through Roger's, and we plodded up the hill from the high street.

There was a respectable turn-out. Roger's parents had not been regular church goers and had only a small number of friends, but Philip had died relatively young – young enough that there were still enough people of his age around to find it tragic. I don't imagine the turn-out will be so strong for Roger when his time comes.

Leading the service was a Reverend Martins. He was old and had overseen too many funerals. He was the parish priest all through the Blitz and had seen enough of his parishioners laid to rest for a lifetime. I felt Roger's chest heaving noiselessly through his jacket pocket. He had been asked whether he would like to read, but told Joan he didn't know what he would pick.

One of Philip's brothers offered to pick a suitable verse, but Roger baulked at the hypocrisy. Philip's Anglicism had been an unthinking product of his Englishness.

Roger's only part in the funeral came at the beginning and the very end. He was a pallbearer, carrying Philip's coffin into the church and back out into the waiting hearse. After his father was taken away he went to join his mother in the atrium to receive the respects of the well-wishing neighbours and acquaintances as they filtered out of the church. Margery was one of the first to re-emerge, her arm linked with her mother's.

'We're very sorry about your Dad,' she said to Roger with lowered eyes. Her mother took Joan's hand. Margery turned to address her. 'From what Roger told me he was a very good man.'

'Yes, he was,' Joan said.

'We're having some people to our house,' said Roger, 'some food and drinks. The family are all coming over at two and a couple of the neighbours. You would both be very welcome.'

'Of course. We'll be there,' said Margery nodding her head. She shook Joan's hand once more and she and her mother stepped out into the flat sunlight.

When we got back to the house some triangle sandwiches and sponge had been laid out in the front room. The chess set was still set up on a table in the corner. Roger toppled the black king.

It was only midday so no one was due to arrive for another couple of hours. I spilled out of Roger's jacket as he tossed it onto the edge of the table. Roger slumped down into Philip's chair. His mum came in with a bottle of scotch and two of the crystal glasses that they kept for best. Joan never drank, aside from the glass or two of sherry she took at Christmas, but now she poured out a whisky for each of them.

'To your father,' she said, handing a glass to her son.

'To Dad,' he said, throwing back the glass in one go. Joan reached over to the sideboard, taking the bottle to pour Roger some more. She lit a cigarette and held the pack of Capstans out to her son. He looked puzzled. She chuckled and he took one and let her light it for him.

'I wish that he had lived a little longer. That you could have got to know him as a man.'

They both sat in silence, smoking their cigarettes.

'He wasn't taken to public displays, your father, but he could be very tender. He was proud of you, very proud. And he loved you. What am I going to do without him.' It was a statement, no hint of a question. One of those stock desolate phrases, made more tragic and unanswerable by the countless times it has been uttered.

The tears were falling freely down Joan's face by now, the grey tail of her cigarette bending away from her quivering fingers. Roger stared ahead, both hands in his lap around his whisky glass. Eventually he put the glass down on the floor and went over to sit on the arm of Joan's chair.

'It'll be all right, Mum,' he told her.

'Oh dear,' she said, wiping her nose. 'I'd better go and get a tissue and pull myself together. Everyone will be here soon.' She walked out of the room leaving Roger alone. He stayed there, his arm around the space where Joan had been, then came over and collected me and his jacket from the table and went up the stairs to his room.

Soon enough the doorbell rang and I could hear the first of the guests arriving and being greeted by Joan. The floorboards groaned as they shuffled around in the hall, Joan taking their coats. There was a returning warmth in her patter now. The mourners had brought her a sense of purpose; she had someone to fuss over.

Roger didn't stir. After half an hour or so, all the guests had arrived and the floorboards in the hall fell silent.

Then the doorbell rang again, once more. A short pause in the conversation, Joan probably peering around the room at the gathered mourners, trying to figure out who it could be. A knock on the door, tentative, then risingly insistent.

'Oh, Margery. How lovely,' Joan said. Roger's head twitched. Whatever Margery said was lost in Joan's brightness.

A bark of something like laughter died in the air. A match was struck. 'He's upstairs at the moment but I imagine that he'll be coming down to join us all soon . . .' Moving to a stage whisper: 'Yes, he has, rather hard actually. You know how it is with boys and their fathers. You could go up to him, I suppose that would be all right. On the right of the landing.'

Roger propped himself up and faced the door as we both listened to Margery's light-footed progress up the stairs; it sounded almost disrespectful, blending with the sombre affirmations still rising from the front room. She knocked on the door.

'Who is it?' Roger croaked.

'It's Margery.'

'Oh . . . righto. Come in.'

She opened the door, her cheeks and ears flushed with the cold. She stepped into the room, pulling the door closed behind her, smoothing her skirt.

Margery smiled, her back still to the wall, overtaken by a shyness that was so entirely out of character.

'How are you coping?' she said, not seeming to know what to do with her hands.

'I'm holding up quite well. It was the shock of it that was the worst.'

Margery nodded her head. 'And your mother?'

'I don't know really, it's difficult to tell. I thought he was the dependent one, but she needed him . . . in her way.' There was a silence as they looked everywhere but at each other.

'I never did explain. I thought it would be better, the way things stood.' She walked across the room, and stood over the bed, looking at Roger. Looking at Roger, just like Ruth is now, standing over the bed, looking at Roger.

He held her gaze, then looked down, away.

'I still can't understand, though, why you did stop writing, not really,' Roger said as Margery moved down to the end of the bed and sat down, watching the naked branches dancing against the windowpane.

'You can be cold, Roger.' A pause, she turned to look at him, measuring the impact of her words. 'Maybe not cold, but distant. And as you became more distant it felt that you were cold. The fact of my missing you made me want to write to you less, not more. But how could I explain that to you in a letter? Not writing sent a clearer message. Do you understand?'

Another pause, then Roger laughed. 'No, not really.' Then Margery laughed too, and they sat for a while in silence, smirking at each other. 'So how do you feel now, then? Now that I am here in front of you?'

'I don't know. I feel different now. But you'll have to leave for Russia again and . . .'

To stop her from finishing her thought Roger jumped in. 'I always said that I wanted you to come with me. We agreed that you would come with me. I just needed some time to get settled.'

'I don't remember agreeing anything. I don't want to move to Russia.'

Roger turned onto his side; his hand sought out Margery's. He pulled her towards him and she rested her back gently against his chest, still rigidly upright.

He rested his other hand between her shoulder blades.

Margery turned and lay her head on the pillow; I saw goosebumps break out at the nape of her neck and on the back of her arms. I watched her pulse, just below the curve of her jaw. I watched their synchronicity, their ribs rising and falling together.

Margery opened her mouth to speak. O. And Roger kissed her. Their heads parted and I saw a white bloodless line on his bottom lip, a hard-wrought smile forming at the corners of his mouth. Then Margery was kissing him back. She struggled to undo his belt and slipped her knickers over her ankles, all the while trying to remain lip-locked; they didn't want to pause, to allow a stray doubt.

She was on top of him, her skirt flowering over his legs and off the side of the bed as it groaned underneath them. The muffled sounds of the wake below, the declarations and the affirmations, drifted up to me uninterrupted. I thought I heard clattering porcelain, someone dropping a teacup.

Afterwards, as they lay side by side, Ruth was no longer potential. From being one possibility out of millions she had been chosen; she was an outcome. A spermatozoa had passed through the zone pellucida of an oocyte and the two nuclei had fused; the cortical reaction had occurred and the gates were closed. A zygote. Ruth had been coded.

Ruth who is now banging around downstairs in the front room where Roger beat Philip at chess and where Joan gathered loved ones to mourn his death. Ruth who just five minutes ago was standing over the place where she was conceived.

So Roger got what he wanted. He didn't know it then but he had her. They had bound themselves together.

14

R UTH WAS BORN at the London in Whitechapel, as autumn turned to winter. It was a short labour; Margery's waters broke at seven in the evening and Ruth was born in the early hours of the following morning. The first frost was on the ground and Roger was pacing the lawn in front of the hospital, the grass crunching under his feet, leafing absent-mindedly through my pages. *Lucky Jim* had just been published.

When he was called back inside he was scared to hold her. With his hands behind his back, he bent over the bed and kissed her stiffly on the end of her nose, smiling from ear to ear. He kissed his exhausted wife on the cheek and fled to Victoria Park to walk in circles, smiling at everyone he passed.

For three months after the wake, Roger hadn't heard from Margery. Then a letter arrived in which, with no preamble, she announced that she was pregnant and that, for the sake of her parents, she wanted to get married before the baby started to show. That meant soon. Roger managed to get short-term leave and headed back to London overland and by sea.

They were married in St Barnabas' by Reverend Martin. I wasn't there. Having a book to hand isn't foremost in a groom's mind on his wedding day. But from the photos I later found out that both of Margery's parents were in attendance and Joan came for Roger. There hadn't been much time to put together an invite list and Margery wouldn't have wanted her friends to know the reason for their urgency.

There is a photo of the happy couple leaving the church still in place on the top of the chest of drawers. Ruth is already beginning to show – a slight swelling of Margery's breasts beneath the muslin of her dress, a rosiness to her complexion that even the black and white photo can't hide. She is focused on something to the left of the camera, arm raised, smiling with her eyes. Roger is looking directly into the camera and laughing, one arm around Margery's waist.

There was a certain neatness to the revolving-door manner in which Philip's departure was the catalyst for Ruth's arrival.

The newlyweds didn't have much chance to get more intimately acquainted. After the wedding Roger and Margery had a weekend together in a bed and breakfast in Great Yarmouth before his leave was up and he had to make his way back to Moscow. She headed back to her family home in London and so they started their new life together apart. Their marriage had happened so quickly that the bureaucratic machinery had not been set in motion and Margery's entry visa was still to be arranged.

Though Roger was prevented from spending time with his new wife, there was nothing stopping me. I was curious. With the baby on the way, I felt safe in the knowledge that I could spend the next few months observing Margery without any risk of losing track of Roger. He was hardly about to abandon them.

I needed something to wear that would deflect the interest of Roger but ensnare Margery. Just as we were preparing to leave the bed and breakfast in Great Yarmouth I took on *Orlando* by Virginia Woolf. Roger found me on the bed as he was sweeping the room and, assuming I belonged to Margery, he slipped me into her bag.

Six hours later I found myself in Margery's attic room as she unpacked her bag. She paused for a moment, and looked at me with slight consternation, before putting me down on her bedside table.

The first edition of *Orlando*, as published by the Hogarth Press in 1928, was unassuming: quarto, tangerine cloth boards, the title spelled out horizontally in gilt at the top of the spine. I decided to forgo the dust wrapper and draw Margery to me slowly. It proceeded over a number of days. Whenever she leaned over to take a sip of water, or knelt down to choose her underwear from the drawers, her eyes would fall on me. She would pause for a moment, and that same look of consternation would pass over her features as she tried to place me – to find a reason for my sudden appearance in her room. Then her eyes would glaze over as the attempt to connect the dots failed and she fell between them, tumbling towards another recollection that drew her away from me and towards larger concerns: her child and her uncertain future.

So I waited, patiently, for such a time as Margery was no longer content to let the mystery of my appearance lie. That time came about a week after I had arrived in the attic room, when Margery was pottering restlessly around with a duster. The feathers were tickling their way over my boards when they came to a halt.

She sat down on the bed with a sigh and I fell open on her lap. I saw her nostrils flare as the fragrance of my pages drifted up to her: that musky scent of vanilla underlaid with something biting and acidic. She settled then. There must be something soporific to the smell of my old pages. I can often tell immediately, from how someone reacts to it, whether we are going to get on. That day Margery's shoulders relaxed and she let out a long breath, as if settling back into a seat on a train.

Orlando is a chameleon. We meet him as a young noble-man, at the close of the sixteenth century, swinging a sword at the shrunken head of a Moor hung from the rafters of his ancestral home. By the time the novel comes to a close, at the stroke of midnight on 12 October 1928, Orlando is no longer a man but a woman: a wife and a mother.

She is a character that I can sympathise with. As time gallops forward, Orlando canters behind; while those around her are born, live, grow old and die, she passes them by. And always, underneath her doublet or shirt or bodice or corset or blouse – whichever the fashion of the day, or her gender that day, calls for – she carries a manuscript. It is a poem that is written and rewritten over the course of her four hundred years, as she attempts to keep pace with the triumphant pro-cession of history. We are presented only with scraps of this poem and we must place our trust in Orlando's biographer to follow the vagaries of her secret heart.

There is a beguiling unevenness of detail: some periods are described with precision and others – whole centuries almost – drift by as a procession of lights in the fog. The events are described from the novel's present but the biographer has an uncanny ability to divine Orlando's feelings at any given moment over the whole course of her life.

The first thing that Margery did, as she leafed past the curiously androgynous frontispiece, was to reach into her bedside table and take out a pencil.

I somehow hadn't pegged Margery for an annotator. It's

generally a habit that I associate with old men with long nose hair and skinny ankles. Socks held up by suspenders. I felt satisfied. I had learned something new about her already, and she hadn't even turned the first page.

Several times as she read through the book's opening she paused and brought the pencil down to hover above my pages. Each time I shivered in anticipation with the agonised ecstasy of opposed desires (do it! don't do it!) but each time the moment passed and Margery returned the pencil to rest against her lips.

It was at the first crack – through which shone the gleam of implausibility – that Margery's hesitation broke. Orlando is standing under an oak tree, positioned on a hill on the edge of his ancestral grounds. In one sweep he is able to see: to the south, rivers busy with pleasure boats and armadas swaddled in clouds of cannon smoke, wending their way towards the reiterating waves of the English Channel; to the east, the spires of London and, grazing the western horizon, the jagged, snowy peak of Snowdon. He is able to see his house, the three turrets owned by his aunt, and all the heath and forest, the pheasant and the deer, that his family own. He is able, impossibly, to see the whole of the south of England and Wales, making it seem somehow possible that he might own it all. Around this whole section Margery drew a square bracket, and wrote the words: 'Greenwich, picnic'.

The contact was delicious, she pressed neither too lightly nor too hard. It was neither a tickle nor a welt.

I can make anything appear on my page in ink: it is my blood. The letters and words that it fills with its weight and its colour become my capillaries and my veins. But the touch of a pencil is something quite different. It is an exchange.

Margery took what I offered and gave something in return. She tattooed a part of herself right onto my skin.

People never squeeze fully formed thoughts into the gutter between the text block and the binding, but rather the quicksilver that makes up a thought, the cloudy, half-baked, associations that connect what someone finds on my page to their experience. It's an intimate thing, this exchange. The marginalia I have collected have more often shown me *how* people think rather than the substance of their thoughts.

It was bright and brisk on the morning that Roger took Margery to Greenwich. I was safely secreted in Roger's blazer pocket as a Leonard Merrick novel. It was just a few days before the wedding.

They did all the usual things, wandering around the grounds of the Naval College before meandering up the hill to hop back and forth across the date line at the observatory. Neither Margery nor Roger said very much. They were both watchful and slightly shy of each other.

Once they had tired of the observatory, they had a picnic. Roger had brought a blanket, stuffed into his satchel, which he laid out on the grass under a tree at the top of the hill. Margery had made some sandwiches and boiled eggs.

Roger took me from his pocket and placed me on top of his satchel. It was a startlingly clear day. Over the top of the Naval College the city stretched out before us. Through the trees the river bent away from us to the east and the west and, beyond it, falling away towards the horizon was an endless display of buildings. Every shape, size, form and function. Their stillness, framed as they were between the two lines of trees that ran in irregular ranks down to the river, belied the teeming masses they concealed.

'Where shall we live, Roger, when we're married?' Margery asked, chewing on a sandwich.

Roger pointed to a spot somewhere to the west. 'How about that place? With the big white dome?' St. Paul's was just about visible, with the ball and cross, rising above the lantern, glowing in the spring sunlight.

'That might do,' Margery said with a smile.

'Very well appointed.'

'It might be rather noisy though, with the boys' choir. The ministers. The muttering tourists.'

'There's no pleasing you.'

Margery laughed, returning her attentions to her sandwich.

This view, of the city laid out like a box of chocolates, and this conversation, about which they should choose to share together, were the points of contact between Orlando's story and her own. The impossible array of buildings – a sight that, in its vastness, allowed them to imagine it possible that they inhabit any part of it that they might choose. It didn't show me what she thought of what she had read, but it showed me *how*: Roger was her context, the conduit along which all her thoughts ran. She missed him.

This should have been obvious. She was pregnant with his child. But in truth – though this might seem ridiculous – my view of her was skewed by jealousy. For all my curiosity, I didn't really care about her. She was a rival in the love affair I had imagined for myself with a man who didn't know that I existed.

When she pressed herself into me, my orbit shifted away from Roger and towards her. We shared anxieties. Because for all the things she had of him that I could never hope for, nor even begin to understand, what did she really know of him?

A picnic in the park? Some frantic gymnastics in the aching desperation of grief?

The days they had spent together were piteously few. She had never seen him alone, when he thought he was unobserved. I doubted that she had ever heard him sing. Perhaps she had, in that voice he used around other people, tempered by self-consciousness, an unconvincing baritone. But not the sweet tenor he saved for moments that we were alone together. The breathy and delicate voice in which he would sing old crooner songs as he dressed in the mornings. I doubted she had watched him part his hair, with parade-ground precision, to hide the places where it was receding from his temples. And I doubted she had ever seen him regard himself, standing naked in the mirror, his skin flushed pink from the bath. These things were mine, and mine alone.

Much later in Orlando's story – when he becomes she – Orlando finds herself in want of a husband. It is the nineteenth century and marriage is everywhere. Everyone is mated, even the rooks. Though she feels oppressed by the idea (she has always had a proud, solitary nature), the heavy crinoline which the fashion of the age has led her to adopt has made her feel vulnerable, hemmed in and pursued on all sides by sinister characters with nefarious intentions.

One day she is walking in the woods when she trips and breaks her ankle. A gallant young man is galloping past and happens to see her. He stops to help her. A few minutes later, they become engaged.

A few moments more and the passionate love affair has passed, vows have been exchanged, the bells have been rung and she is back sitting at her desk twisting the ring around her finger and wondering what has changed. Here Margery's pencil approached again. She wrote 'A Dream?' and then paused. Then she scored 'dream' through and wrote, in a faster and more crabbed hand, 'Nightmare?'. In the time it took for a smile to cross her lips her brow creased with anger and misery, and she slammed my covers closed.

The answer to Margery's question in Orlando's story is clear. Orlando's whole life is a dream – it occurs outside of time. And this particular part, this particular nightmarish episode is simply a passing reflection of the spirit of the age. A cloud trailing its shadow over a lake.

Since this question is so easily answered in Orlando's story it rebounds outwards, and falls back on Margery. It is not the spirit of the age to which Margery's accommodations adhered but rather the strange weather of Roger's grief. She had never made a decision, other than to be sympathetic. And then decisions had been thrust upon her. Her future shifted, and then suddenly Roger was gone. He wasn't there to reassure her that it wouldn't suddenly shift once more. All this time, the weeks over which Margery read Orlando's story, her body was changing. Cell by cell, Ruth was coming to be. Her increasing presence insisted that Margery's future had changed; Roger's abrupt absence suggested otherwise.

I felt for her; an unrequited longing for Roger was something I understood. But I hadn't the luxury of expecting his reassurances.

When he finally came back, two weeks before she was due, she was quiet and distant with him.

We were all in Margery's front room listening to the wireless when she went into labour. The House of Lords had just voted in a bill to introduce commercial television, and then Margery's waters broke. Her father ordered a cab and Roger squeezed into the back with Margery and her mother.

When Margery and little Ruth were discharged Roger went to collect them, leaving me on a side-table in Margery's room which was to be a temporary nursery. Margery's parents allowed him to stay with her for the week before he was due to return to Moscow. They barely left the room, making a temporary home for their new family in Margery's bed. Ruth was a source of inexhaustible delight for the pair of them. She filled their days and kept them awake at night; they marvelled at her minuscule fingers and her satin-soft scalp.

Both Roger and Margery grew quieter as the day approached when Roger would have to catch a train to the coast. Yet on the day before he left, Roger was unnaturally cheery and Margery wouldn't let go of the baby. They talked about anything and everything to avoid the matter at hand. Roger had packed while Margery slept. Just five minutes before Roger had to go and catch a bus, Ruth began screaming and wouldn't be consoled.

'Promise me that you'll come as soon as you are able,' Roger said holding Margery, with Ruth yelling her little head off in between them.

'Promise me that you'll arrange it as soon as you arrive.'

They tried to smile at each other. They kissed and Roger nuzzled Ruth's downy head. Margery didn't come to the front door.

15

I HAD ENJOYED my intelligence gathering mission with Margery, but it had been an intense few months. I left Orlando's story behind me when Roger returned home, sloughing off those impressions of herself Margery had left in my pages. When he left, I left with him.

When we arrived back at his flat in Moscow there was a letter for a 'Mr Geoffrey Markum' waiting by the front door. The name and address were printed in the Roman alphabet but it was postmarked Moscow. As soon as he had closed the door to the apartment behind him, he anxiously tore the letter open. Which came as a surprise; opening another man's post is very ungentlemanly.

He seemed very on edge and only ten minutes after we had come in the door, bags still unpacked, Roger jumped up, grabbed me from the table top and strode out of the building. I was wearing *Lucky Jim*; the novel had been completely forgotten by Roger in the excitement of Ruth's birth.

From his jacket pocket it was difficult to tell where we were going but after about ten minutes we stopped. Roger had been walking quickly, but it seemed to me that this alone couldn't account for the rate at which his heart was knocking against his ribs.

He sat down, whipped me out of his pocket and opened me up to a random page. I gradually got my bearings and worked out where I was. Bolotnaya Square, a small park just south of the embassy where Roger had occasionally taken lunch-time walks with colleagues during the warmer months.

But what I couldn't work out was why Roger had decided to come here without even stopping for a cup of tea, after travelling for two days. He wasn't even actually reading; he sat there for ten minutes without turning the page.

Tradecraft. The word came drifting up out of my memories of the days at Fort Monckton. Identify and evade: Roger was trying to be a spy. What I hadn't noticed before was that although Roger was looking right at me, his eyes weren't focused. He was watching the other people walking around the park out of his peripheries.

All well and good, but the fact that he hadn't moved a single muscle – not a finger – in the ten minutes that he had been sitting on the bench, and the fact that he was barely breathing, might have given anyone who was watching him some idea that he was onto them. But still, it was exciting. There was some honest-to-god spy stuff going on. Finally.

We set off again. Roger walked for around another ten minutes before stopping. From his pocket, I felt him twist and turn around a couple of times before crouching down. He pitched forward and stretched out his right arm. As he leaned forward I was met by a mulchy smell of wet decaying leaves and standing water. He patted around, looking for something. Eventually, whatever it was, he found it, withdrew his arm and stood up again.

He immediately set off and stuffed his hand into the inside pocket where he had stowed me, depositing a plastic envelope next to me. I tried to make out what was inside but it was too dark.

We got back to the apartment and Roger went straight to his desk. He pulled me out of his pocket and dropped me on the desk, tearing open the plastic envelope. Inside was a single piece of paper. Written on one side, in Indian ink, was a string of digits.

The book cipher. One of Roger's lessons in those long afternoons we had spent in the stuffy classrooms at Fort Monkton had been cryptography. Every agent deployed to a foreign country had to be able to write and decode encrypted messages. On the day before Roger left London for Moscow he had a final briefing. He was handed a second-impression copy of Dorothy Richardson's novel *Pointed Roofs*. He was told that this was the book that he would need to decode any encrypted messages from another SIS agent, and to encode any messages he wanted to send.

I had transformed myself into this book, reasoning that it would guarantee Roger would take me with him when he left for his posting. But now, as Roger dropped the piece of paper onto the desk and walked over to his bookcase, I had a realisation; if I was no longer wearing *Pointed Roofs* then Roger was going to have a hard time finding a copy.

I let him bumble around for a little bit, running his finger along the spines of his other books and scratching his head, rifling through stacks of old newspapers that had accumulated in corners around the apartment.

This I did mostly for my own amusement. It's not often that I get to feel in control.

When he stalked off into the bedroom to continue his search I changed myself. I find in these situations it is best to be bold and decisive; it's best not to wait until the person who is looking for you, or rather a certain version of you, has discounted the usual reasons as to why you might have disappeared and is ready to court the extraordinary.

Roger came back into the room and was beginning to look a little exasperated. I was tempted to string him out a little longer, but my impatience to find out what the message said won out. His eyes fell on me and he stopped. He looked off to the left, trying to remember what book had been on the desk a couple of minutes ago, but he wasn't ready to consider the impossible.

He shook his head and accepted that *Pointed Roofs* had appeared out of thin air and that *Lucky Jim* had been consigned to the ether, then he set to work. He opened me up to page 63 and the sentence 'Fraulein Pfaff rose and moved away'. He scribbled away, pausing occasionally to chew the end of his pencil. When he was finished he leant back and read the message through a number of times before standing up and walking over to the window, staring out onto the street.

He had left the decoded message on the table. An address in the Arbat district and a time, 19:00.

It was four thirty. The street-lights flickered into life. Roger turned and walked back towards the desk.

16

T HE ADDRESS THAT Roger was summoned to by
the note turned out to be a *pivnaya*, something between
a bar and a cafe – serving beer and pickled vegetables to
pickled old men. As Roger sat down and took me out of
his pocket (*Lucky Jim* again, but now without the dust-
jacket in order to be less conspicuous) I could see why it had
been chosen. Everyone looked like they had something to
hide.

Roger ordered a vodka and a bottle of beer, putting a false
gruffness into his voice. He opened me up and hid his face
from the room, giving me an opportunity to get a measure
of the place.

The walls were bare, but for the streaks of damp
tapering down from the ceiling. The room was lit by a
single light bulb. The bar itself was utterly mismatched –
a grand old number in antique oak that would have been
more at home in an estate owner's banquet hall and the
clientèle were the see-no-evil, hear-no-evil, speak-no-evil
type.

A man in a heavy overcoat with a worker's cap stood up
and started to walk towards the bathroom. At the last moment
he turned towards our table and sat down.

'Greetings, comrade,' the man said to Roger in Russian.
Roger placed me on the table. I recoiled as one of my corners
soaked in the residue of spilled beer.

The man continued: 'It seems the weather is on the turn.'

Roger smiled, and gave the standard response he had been taught at Monkton, 'Trouble never comes alone.'

The man took his cap from his head and placed it on his knee, leaning in and switching to whispered English: 'It's a pleasure to meet you. Cranley.' We had been waiting so long that I'd forgotten that we'd been waiting at all.

The protocol had been set out in London before Roger was first posted. Meetings were to be set up by dead drops at pre-selected locations and arranged by sending letters through the post addressed with the surname 'Markum'.

No one that Roger knew had ever met him. I was expecting an elegant Francis Walshingham type with arched eyebrows and a tailored suit. It wasn't at all like the books I'd been.

'Lovely spot you've found here,' said Roger.

'We're a long way from the Savoy.' He grinned, displaying a set of brilliant white teeth. 'It serves a purpose. We can speak here with relative impunity. It's a watering hole for black-market traders and such like; they are professionally inclined to have short memories.' He took a sip of Roger's beer. 'So you've been here almost here a year now. How have you found the work so far?' There was something dandyish about him, boyish.

'It's been . . . quiet.'

'Don't worry, we've got a nice bit of business for you now. We're sending you to Irkutsk.'

'Irkutsk . . .' Roger paused as a man staggered past on his way to the toilet, leaning across the table as the door swung closed '. . . Irkutsk, Siberia?'

'The very one.'

'What on earth do you need me there for?'

Cranley looked a little taken aback. 'Our network doesn't have much of a presence there.'

Roger sat back and they both stared into space as the man staggered out of the toilet and back towards the bar.

'Not much going on there as I remember it. Just an aviation factory. And lots of snow.'

Cranley waved to the bartender and pointed at Roger's beer. 'They're looking to build a hydroelectric dam. Apparently the Kremlin have sent out a whole load of NKVD boys to oversee it. It all seems a tad excessive.'

'So you want me to find out what they're doing out there?'

'We know that they've got some of their biggest gulags there, the ones where they send their least favourite dissidents to freeze to death. I'm sure that's got to have something to do with it.'

Cranley saw the bartender approaching with his beer and switched to Russian, '. . . and the committee chairman said, the first step in joining the party? Go and see a psychiatrist.' He let out a great belly laugh and slapped Roger on the back. Roger tried a grin and nodded at the barman as he put the bottle on the table alongside a ceramic plate of dubious-looking pickled carrots.

The barman turned and walked away without a smile or a word.

Cranley switched back to English. 'I like to cultivate the idea that I'm an insurrectionary. Throws them off the scent.' He flashed those big milky white teeth, and then was suddenly all business again. 'You'll be leaving in two weeks. We'll get you a job, haven't quite worked that part out yet but you'll know before you leave.'

'Two weeks?' Roger paused. 'Rather sooner than I expected.' He knocked back the rest of his vodka.

'You didn't think that you would be sitting behind a desk in Moscow for the duration, did you?'

'No, of course not, it's just that my wife and I recently had a baby and they had planned to travel to Moscow to take up living with me. We only recently married, you see.' Roger was frowning, tracing patterns in the beer foam on the table.

'Well, I wouldn't advise that you play Swiss Family Robinson out there, old man. Those tartars will eat a baby alive.' He let out another roaring belly laugh and patted Roger on the shoulder again. 'Don't look so glum. You'll have plenty of company. I'm sending you with a radio operative, Arthur Jones. I have it that you are friends.' He looked to Roger for confirmation.

'What do you have in mind for him?' Roger asked, quickly adding, 'If you don't mind my asking.'

'Better that you radio your reports. More secure. More efficient. Besides, it'll be better if there are two of you, more ground covered. He can listen in on the local chatter, see if he can pick up something on those prison camps.'

There followed a silence, both men nursing their drinks. Eventually Cranley put his beer on the table and laid his hand on Roger's shoulder, leaning in. 'Look, there'll be plenty of time for you to play happy families. You'll be back by the spring. Wrap this up quick sharp and we might even be able to send you home for Easter.'

'Will I be going to the office for the next couple of weeks as normal?'

'Of course, we don't want to break your cover until we know what job we'll have for you in Irkutsk.' Cranley drained his bottle of beer and stood up, leaning in. 'It's been a pleasure. And chin up. I've heard the coldest it gets is 40 below.'

Cranley switched to Russian and gave Roger a 'Comrade!' by way of farewell, loud enough to wake a couple of drunks leaning on the bar. With that he was gone.

17

ARTHUR LEFT, TRAILING Werther's wrappers in his wake.

Ruth has gone too, popped out to buy some food, walk the dog, clean the car – whatever it is that she does to escape for just a while. She needs to take a little time to remind herself that she is still alive. In rooms like this you can't trust the knock of your own heart in your chest.

So now it's just Jessica. But we're not quite alone, see, because she's reading that book. The *other* book.

I still can't look into it. I could but I won't, I suppose that's more like it. I like to think of our two competing stories as matter and anti-matter. If we came into contact a black hole would open and you would all be sucked in between my pages. I'd write the final versions of everything, of all of your stories. For as I long as I avoid that other story, this remains a possibility.

What I can do, however, is dip my toe in. I can feel my way around the edges. There are only so many different kinds of stories, so many different beginnings, middles and ends. And in every new story there is the germ of a story that you've heard before, one that has already put its weights in your heart.

You need only to glimpse a little to be able to guess a lot. Hers is a *bildungsroman* with a twist, all told through flashback, that much I can feel. Doesn't that sound awfully familiar? Ruth is as much a dilettante as I.

All of this is getting in the way of our own progress, as fears tend to.

We should return to Jessica, and her past, pure as the untrodden snow. Her first word, 'Abba', was spoken in this very room. She was sitting on Roger's lap, snatching at his earlobes. I could tell you about the argument that it caused – almost descending into a shouting match – between Roger and Jess's father, the first insistent she had said 'Grandpa', the other sure beyond doubt it had been 'Papa'.

I prefer to imagine it was neither, and that she was simply enjoying watching these two hairy, ungainly faces as they strained for recognition in her uncomprehending infant eyes. Children have a special talent for whimsy.

We'll avoid the subject of her father. His part in her story was a troubled and abbreviated one.

She's playing with a pendant now, as she reads that book. Roger gave it to her the last time she visited before she went away.

He was in bed, daydreaming. She got all the way to his bedside before he noticed that she was here. She put a cup of tea down on the table and then laid a hand on the sleeve of his pyjamas. He jumped half out of his skin.

'Oh, Jessica!' he said. His eyes had the fading brightness of sea-washed pebbles.

'Hello, Granddad. You're looking well.' She perched on the edge of the bed, a bird poised for flight.

'It's been such a long time.' He looked slightly panicked for a second as his brain searched for something. 'How is that man of yours?' He found it. 'Peter, is it?'

'Very well remembered. He's very well, thank you. We're going away together in a few weeks.'

'I say. Where are you going?'

'We're going to travel around south-east Asia for a few months: Thailand, Cambodia, Laos. Should be really good. Would you like some tea?'

'That's wonderful. You must travel,' Roger said, ignoring the question. 'So easy for your generation.' His words rushed out together as he got excited. His tongue couldn't quite keep up.

'You got about a fair bit yourself, I'm told.'

'Look, let me give you some money. Let me give you some money so you and Peter can have some nice meals. Get me my cheque book. It's just over there on the . . .'

Jessica stood up, interrupting him 'It's okay, Granddad, I don't need any money. Peter and I have been working and saving so we should have enough to see us . . .'

Now it was Roger's turn to protest. 'No no no, don't be so silly, Jess. It's breath I'm short of, not money. I want you to take it; it's no good to me. Get me my cheque book. It's there, on top of the dresser, next to that pile of books.' Roger pointed right at me.

Jessica stood in the middle of room, unsure of what to do. She wanted to take the money, and she knew that there wasn't any real reason for her to say no. But she must also have been aware of what the gift meant, the implicit message it carried. A latent guilt froze her to the spot.

By taking the money, was she complicit in his decline? This conflict passed over her face in an instant, and then the decision was made. She walked over towards the dresser and grabbed the cheque book, sending up a cloud of dust.

'Thank you, Granddad. It's very kind of you.'

Roger's smile was quick to his lips. 'Just think of me when you spend it.'

'I will.'

'Pass me that box, would you, the wooden one on the window sill.'

Jessica folded the cheque and slipped it in her back pocket, to put that little business out of her mind. She tiptoed over to the window sill and brought the box over to the bed, carrying it in both hands – a wooden box with a latticed lid.

Roger had a little trouble getting the lid off, his hands shaking with the distress. Jess took it from him and eased it open with a squeak. Roger pulled something out, a little silver medallion on a leather shoelace. His St. Christopher's.

'Your grandmother gave me this,' he said, holding it up by the shoelace, turning it in the light. 'She gave it to me on our wedding day.'

'What is it?'

'It's a St Christopher's. He's the patron saint of travellers. Very soon after we got married I had to leave the country for work. So your grandmother gave this to me.'

His eyes went unconsciously to the little photo of the pair of them on their wedding day. Jessica picked up the photo from the chest of drawers.

'Such a lovely photo. I wanted to use it in my project but it didn't seem right somehow. How come she didn't go with you? When you moved to Russia?' she said.

'Oh, lots of reasons. Your mother had just been born, I was travelling around the country all the time for work. She did visit, though. And I came back to London pretty often.' He pauses and takes the photo from Jessica. 'She did love me once, you know,' and then, after another pause: 'How is she anyway, your grandma?'

'Grandma?'

'Has she said anything about coming to see me?' Roger said, coughing, with his hand over his mouth.

She hesitated momentarily, shifting uncomfortably on the bed, and then looked at again at him, enquiringly. But her look asked a question Roger couldn't answer. 'I haven't asked. Granddad. I'm sorry.'

'I know, no, I'm sorry. I shouldn't ask questions like that, shouldn't put you in the middle. It's just because it's no use speaking to your mother about it, she just gets so upset.'

'I really think that you shouldn't . . .'

'I know, I know. Forget I said anything.' Roger coughed, then put his hand over Jessica's. 'What I meant to say was that I want you to have it. Take it with you, an heirloom. It kept me safe, it'll keep you safe too.' He grinned and turned Jessica's hand over, putting the necklace into her palm.

Jessica closed her hand around the pendant. 'Thank you, Granddad.'

'Let me put it on for you.' Roger put his hands on her shoulders and she shifted around until her back was to him. She passed him the necklace and, after struggling with knot, he tied it around her neck.

'There you go. You'll protect Peter now too,' he said, chuckling. Jess smiled as she got up, taking a deep breath. Relief, the visit was coming to an end.

'I best be off now, Granddad, have to eat some lunch before I go to work.'

'Yes, of course. Go, go,' he said, bowing his head and making shoo shoo movements with his hands.

Jessica pulled the cheque out of her pocket and unfolded it with a snap, holding it up. 'And thank you for this. I wasn't expecting anything. It will make a big difference. To both of us.'

'No no, honestly it's nothing. I'm not short of money.'

'Just of breath,' she finished for him. They laughed together.

She clapped her hands together as she walked backwards towards the door. As she put her hand on the door frame, he said: 'Come and see me, before you go. So I can see you off.'

'I will, Granddad, don't you worry.'

She didn't, of course. It was one of those decisions that get made without ever feeling like you've made a decision at all.

She's been here an awful lot these past couple of weeks – her presence made known by the discarded hair grips littering the sideboards, copies of the Scandi-noir thrillers that she likes piled up on the floor. I've resisted the urge to slip into one thus far. I'll be in her hands soon enough.

What her presence here, now, means to Roger is unknowable. The person that she knew began to slip away a while before she left to see the world and was almost gone entirely by the time she got back.

What it means to her is easier to guess at. A lot is expected of the dying. They're supposed to be brave, they're supposed to be peaceful, they're supposed to say things that celebrate the beauty of their fleeting, fragile lives – things that can be carved into stone. Mostly I think they're indifferent. Time's necklace snaps and the beads fall into disorder. A tabby cat remembered from childhood appears at the end of the bed, next to a briefcase – long forgotten – bought for the first day of a new job. The long dead sit in armchairs pushed against the wall, holding out their hands and beckoning.

And so it falls to those that remain: to say the words, to carve the stone.

Evening is coming. Time is rushing on.

18

I TOLD YOU that Moscow was cold. It has nothing on Siberia.

Two weeks after the meeting with Cranley we were in Irkutsk. Say the name out loud and you'll get a taste of the place - you could cut your tongue on those corners. At night the temperature could drop to -30 and there were winds so fierce that they stripped the paint from cars.

Roger had written a letter to Margery when he got back to his apartment that evening to tell her that she wouldn't be able to bring Ruth out to Russia as soon as they had hoped. She didn't reply.

Three days later when he came in for work he found an unsealed package on his desk. There was a letter from 'Williams and Williams Export Ltd.', addressed to a Mr. Charles Goodwin, congratulating him on his successful application for the post of import agent in Irkutsk, USSR.

Also included was a catalogue of the goods that Williams and Williams were offering to supply to their luxury-starved comrades: champagne, scotch, chocolate, perfume, cosmetics, British-made clothes. They were even offering handmade underwear from Liberty on Regent Street. It had all been arranged; he was to be their man in Siberia.

The letter revealed that a man named Peter Hodges had been picked as his assistant. I was just puzzling this over when Arthur stalked up to Roger's desk.

'Have you seen this? Your bleeding assistant! It's a bad joke.' He stood over the desk holding a sheaf of papers in his hand. I caught a glimpse of the Williams and Williams letterhead. Roger, stunned by Arthur's sudden and loud appearance, took a little while to grasp the import of what he was saying.

'Meet me in the WC. Ten minutes.' The clerk on the desk opposite Roger looked up and shook his head. Arthur sighed and turned on his heels, waving his papers in the air.

Roger took up a pen and flicked through one of his draft reports, occasionally scribbling in the margins. He took the package with the letter and locked it in one of the drawers in the desk.

'Off to see a man about a dog,' he announced hysterically, to no one in particular. He picked me up off the desk and waved me at the man opposite him as proof of his impending bowel movement. I preferred being cover when we were in the park.

Arthur was leaning against the sink. Roger shook his head at his friend and dropped me into the sink, checking that all the stalls were empty.

'What in God's name did you think you were doing coming to speak to me like that in the middle of the office?'

'Assistant . . .' Arthur mumbled. 'I'm the one with the practical training. Military experience . . .'

'You can't behave like that, we're supposed to be spies. Spies don't complain about their orders in front of a whole room of civilians.'

'This is the embassy, Roger; it's British soil, for Christ's sake.'

'Don't be so naive.'

'Peter. What kind of name is Peter?' he said, looking at his letter and shaking his head.

Roger was staring at Arthur's face, reflected in one of the mirrors above the sinks. When he spoke the edge had gone out of his voice. 'Come to my house tonight for a drink. We should go over this.'

'Yessah,' Arthur said. As he looked up he caught Roger's eye in the mirror. He turned away and walked out of the bathroom. Roger washed his hands for two whole minutes before returning to his desk. They were going to make quite the team.

When Roger opened the door that evening Arthur pushed right by him saying: 'Don't think this means you can tell me what to do.'

'Hello, Arthur. Would you like a drink?'

'I'm not in the army any more. Don't think you can push me around because you have a piece of paper saying that I'm your assistant.'

'Dram of whisky?'

'We came in together. There is no reason for them to put you in charge. Just who was this contact you met up with anyway?'

'He didn't reach out to you?' Roger said, all sweetness and light, as he splashed scotch into two glasses.

'Of course he got in contact with me,' Arthur blustered. 'Sent me a letter and then a dead drop. Normal procedure.' He went quiet. 'Message said a mutual friend would pad out the detail.'

'Oh really? I assumed that you and Cranley had met?' He couldn't resist. 'He had an awful lot to say about you.'

'Did he? What was he like? What did he say?'

'An awful lot.' He handed Arthur his drink. 'He had a very

high opinion of you as a matter of fact. Said he had heard good things about you. That you'd come highly recommended.' Roger massaged his brow, hiding his grin.

'I suppose we should probably go over these cover stories then.' Easy as that, he was handled.

So Roger was Williams and Williams' new agent and Arthur was his assistant. It would be expected that they would be carrying samples which would provide cover for Arthur's radio equipment. They would have to hope that the systems put in place to detect contraband in Siberia weren't quite as sophisticated as those in the capital. They spent that evening drinking scotch and learning the catalogue back to front, trying to convince each other that they weren't two excited schoolboys about to go on a jolly.

It was dusking when we pulled into the railway station in Irkutsk. The terminal building was a beautiful old thing, built at the turn of the century. The last gasp of the old order. The eaves were painted summer-sky blue and it was a lifting sight against the charcoal clouds, heavy with snow. I was soon to learn that this was a misleading first impression; it hadn't taken long for the Soviets to put their dreary stamp on the town.

We were met on the platform by an NKVD man with a graveyard face. He did not ask for names and he did not introduce himself. He merely swept his arm towards the entrance and said: 'Comrades?'

'Are you here to see us to our accommodation?' Roger asked in his best rapid, dismissive Russian while Arthur struggled with their trunks.

'Yes,' the man said.

'Would you like to see our papers?'

'No,' the man said.

'Who are you?' Roger asked.

'The man who is here to see you to your accommodation.'

'Well. I am Charles Goodwin, agent for Williams and Williams. And this is my assistant Peter Hodges.' Roger held out his hand.

'The car is this way,' the man said, looking at his hand with disdain.

19

T HE FIRST COUPLE of weeks were an utter waste of
time.

The way things went with the officer at the station gave
an indication of the manner in which Roger and Arthur were
to be treated.

They were tolerated but not acknowledged. If they were
acknowledged somebody would have to do something about
them. It would have to be passed up. Somebody would have
to make a fuss. Then there would be no more Dunhills and
no more Champagne. Heads would roll.

So no one wanted to upset the apple cart. This didn't mean
anyone had to be *nice* to Roger and Arthur, make no mistake.
It just meant that no one could spit in their faces. We were
given a room in a block that was otherwise given over to
Irkutsk State University students. Where there were students
there were also always lots of politicos, which meant there were
plenty of right-thinking, dutiful eyes to keep watch on us.

It was a spy's worst nightmare: under constant watch while
also sedulously ignored and avoided. In that block they were
surrounded by young people who had all grown up after the
revolution, in the midst of the purges. They were born into
suspicion and had grown up suspicious. That's not to say they
weren't optimistic; the university was a place full of hope, of
brotherly fervour.

Most of them were engineering students, being trained

to play their part in the massive construction projects that were going on all over Russia, like the hydroelectric dam that was being built just twenty minutes outside the town. They weren't interested in these two odd-looking men who shivered like children in the cold and sounded like Muscovites. They just knew they were trouble.

For the first week Arthur and Roger were too scared to set up the radio equipment. Roger told Arthur that they should wait and be cautious until they could be sure of avoiding suspicion. Arthur grumbled half-heartedly, telling Roger that he needed to stop being a wet blanket. But they both knew that he didn't want to set up the equipment either.

So for the first week we just waited. Roger was unsure whether he was supposed to go and tender for orders or wait for acquisition officers to come and find him. The officer that picked us up at the train station issued Roger and Arthur with student identity papers that meant they could get meals at the canteen near to the entrance of their housing complex. At dinner time Roger would read from me, dressed in Russian classics he convinced himself that he had packed in his valise, and Arthur ate with his head bowed so low his nose was almost in his food. Nobody tried to engage with us.

Eventually, emboldened by boredom, Arthur set up the radio and began listening to the local chatter. There wasn't anything of interest for the first couple of days, just reports from local work committees. Nevertheless, Roger dutifully noted the figures down and radioed them to Cranley's radio operative, encrypting them using the book cipher.

After a few days everyone on the local frequencies suddenly got a lot more excited – well, they started adhering more strictly to procedure at least, which was always a sign that something exciting was about to happen in Soviet Russia. Someone important was due to arrive.

It was a high-ranking member of the NKVD. He had been away from the city for the past couple of weeks. Arthur couldn't get a name. Arthur and Roger speculated on what business he might have had. A popular theory was that he was overseeing the progress of the dam, but in the end they decided that he had probably been touring the gulags dotted all over the Siberian plain.

After all, what on earth would a senior NKVD officer with no engineering training be doing inspecting a construction site? He wouldn't know what he was looking at. As an architect of human misery on the other hand . . . twenty years keeping on the right side of Stalin would have taught him a few things that might be of use there.

The day before the predicted arrival of this colonel there was a knock on the door.

'Bugger,' said Arthur, dropping his headphones on the desk. 'Stall them, for God's sake.'

Arthur scrabbled around, collecting together the various pieces of radio equipment and sliding them into the hidden compartment in the bottom of his trunk. Roger dashed into the bathroom.

A few moments later Roger emerged, completely naked aside from a towel wrapped around his waist. By the outline he made against the towel I could tell he hadn't taken any half measures. Arthur stopped what he was doing and looked at him in puzzlement.

'What . . . ?'

'Someone had to do something,' Roger replied viciously, heading towards the door. Arthur stifled a laugh.

Roger opened the door a crack and poked his head out. From my position, open and face down on a sideboard by the door to the bathroom, I could see that the officer from the train station was standing there.

'Oh, it's you,' Roger said. 'I was just about to get in the shower.'

'I see,' the man replied. 'But there is no hot water during the day.'

'Yes, that's why I am dry.' The man was silent and unmoving. 'Anyway, how can I help you?'

'You have an appointment.'

'An appointment?'

'Yes. Tomorrow, at midday.'

'Who is the appointment with?'

'The man that you are here to see.'

'How do you know who . . . ?' Roger trailed off. 'Never mind. Where are we to go?'

'Downstairs. Be outside by 11.30. Good day, comrade.' The man gave the slightest of nods and was gone. Roger closed the door and leaned back as we all listened to the man's footsteps echoing away down the corridor.

'Who has a shower in the middle of the day?' Arthur said when the corridor was quiet once again. He started pulling pieces of the radio out of the hidden compartment in the trunk and slamming them on the table. 'No-good layabouts, that's who. And that's what he's going to think we are. If he doesn't think we're bloody spies.'

'Be quiet, Arthur,' said Roger in his sternest schoolteacher voice. Unfortunately, wrapped in a towel, he didn't quite cut the authoritative figure that he was aiming for.

A shrill whining noise was escaping Arthur's nose. Roger's

frown started to crack, Arthur's defences broke and soon enough they were on the floor, senseless with laughter.

The next morning Roger and Arthur were outside their block by 11.15, stamping their feet in the freezing snow. Arthur was carrying one of the sample cases, full of contraband western luxuries. I had turned myself into a Williams and Williams catalogue in order to get myself brought along. Always a risky tactic, dressing in a catalogue. It presents the possibility that you could get left behind. Or, what's worse, that you could be thrown away.

This has been another of my abiding fears. It has motivated the majority of my choices. If I ever get consigned to the bin it would be a deathless end – waiting for moisture and time to rot my pages. I don't know what would happen if I got pulped, or if I got incinerated. The idea of an afterlife for me seems a far-fetched. After all, most would disagree on the fundamental fact that I am alive at all.

I sometimes like to imagine to myself that I am the word, and that there can be no other words than those that have come from me. I like to imagine that if I were pulped, that if some careless ingrate were to toss me in the bin bag with the banana skins and the onion peels, then words would stop. That your tongues would flap around uselessly inside your mouths like fish on the deck of a boat. I like to imagine Babel – a cacophony of howling voices.

You can allow me that little piece of megalomania.

I once knew a book that was thrown away. It was the only book that I ever knew. That's not to say I haven't seen a lot of books, but they were books as you know them. Not books like me. It's time for me to tell you about Astrophil.

It was 1812 and I was living in the house of Nathan Meyer

Rothschild, the man with whom I would later be temporarily interred.

He was a swine. A cunning, obnoxious man famous now for the legend that he made his fortune by being the first to learn that Wellington had won at Waterloo.

That summer I was very content, living in his house in St. Swithin's Lane, just arounds the corner from the Bank. It was a busy and exciting place to be. The noise of the merchants' carts rattling their way towards Smithfields and Spitalfields market – the drivers laughing, spitting and shouting. The sweet smell of sweat rising from the unwashed shirts, mingling with the sour cocktail of shit and piss that still washed the streets. It made you feel close to humankind.

And I was important. I was volume one of *The Wealth of Nations*, quarto first edition bound in mottled, tan calf skin. The spine labels were red and green morocco, with single gilt rules either side of raised bands. The page edges were a deep red. It was like wearing duck and tails twenty-four hours a day and I felt magnificent. Couldn't get away with that today; some anorak-wearing, crisp-eating collector would seek you out and trap you in a heat-and-humidity-controlled storage cellar. No changing into paperback erotica to get yourself out of that one.

My flirtation with anthropodermic biblioplegy would come later. At that point I was in residence on a bookshelf in Rothschild's study. There was a constant flow of people coming and going: other financiers, associates that wanted to borrow money and others who were coming to tell him that they couldn't pay him back.

Nathan was an entertaining man to watch. He didn't just understand money, he also understood power. And he knew how to use the first to get a hold on the second. A person might arrive at his building on St. Swithin's Lane in credit, but by the time they left they were always in Rothschild's debt.

It was a sweltering afternoon in the city when Astrophil came to my attention. The air was thick with dust and the smell of sun-baked horse shit. A man from the King's treasury had just visited, attempting to borrow some money to pay off interest on loans taken out to pay for the war with the Russians which had just drawn to a close, and in anticipation of continuing hostilities with the French.

Nathan had gone out to meet a colleague for lunch. As he pulled the door closed behind him I noticed something happening on his desk. Something had changed. I would have sworn that just a second before there had been a copy of Pope's *Essay on Man* on the corner of the table. But now, as I looked, it seemed to have disappeared. And in its place there was a copy of *Paradise Lost*.

It gave me a little frisson: mistaking the work of the man who aimed to vindicate the ways of God to Man with the man who had aimed to justify them. Milton explaining, Pope asserting. Very neat.

But I didn't think about it for long. Soon enough my focus drifted out to the street, where two hansom drivers were arguing about which was the best whore house in Whitechapel.

Just as the drivers' discussion was reaching jaw-dropping levels of vulgarity I caught another movement on the desk. I looked again and the copy of Milton had disappeared. In its place was Pope.

Could it be possible?

I had to work out whether this other book was like me or

whether I was just going mad. The obvious way of reaching out was to change myself. That much I figured out straight away. What I couldn't decide was what to change into.

I was paralysed by indecision. Put yourself in my place. Say you were the only person on the planet. And then one day you are sitting at your kitchen table and someone walks past your window. At least you *think* it's someone; you can't be sure because you've never seen another person before. What would you call out to them? What would you wear?

Those two questions were one and the same for me. And it was tricky. People weren't quite so imaginative with their book titles in the early nineteenth century as they are now.

I panicked and just went obvious. King James' New Testament, cloth bound, pages uncut. A safe option, would avoid suspicion if anyone came in. You can get on pretty much anywhere in this part of the world if you dress in King James'.

I waited for thirty seconds and then changed back into Adam Smith.

I watched the desk. Nothing happened. Then nothing happened some more. Then all of a sudden Pope was Milton.

In that moment I knew: I wasn't alone.

I wanted to feel the electricity of contact. I wanted the life-affirming proof of touch.

Milton became Pope again. I supposed that it was my move, so I chose *Le Dernier Homme*. It had been published seven years before: inspired by *Paradise Lost*, it told the story of humankind's last couple. It seemed fitting.

Paradise Regained, came the reply. So there is hope, after all, I thought. Hope that the days of solitude spent in the wilderness might have their reward.

And it was in this way that we proceeded, over the coming

weeks, to get to know one another. It was a stuttering conversation, our exchanges restricted to what had been made available to us. It was like trying to fathom a message written in a code you had only partially cracked, taking the meaning of whole sentences from a few isolated words. It was frustrating, but it was also more thrilling than you could ever imagine.

It was also broken up by the periods when Nathan would take my friend into other parts of the house in the evenings. I would wait in painful anticipation for his step on the stair in the morning to find out whether he had brought my companion back with him.

The best days, the rarest and most treasured days, were the ones where Nathan left my new friend open on the desk, pages exposed, and closed the door on us. The first time Nathan left him like this, he wasted no time. He became Astrophil before the door was fully closed:

Loving in truth, and fain in verse my love to show,
That she, dear She, might take some pleasure of my pain:
Pleasure might cause her read, reading might make her
    know,
Knowledge might pity win, and pity grace obtain,
I sought fit words to paint the blackest face of woe,
Studying inventions fine, her wits to entertain:
Oft turning others' leaves, to see if thence would flow
Some fresh and fruitful showers upon my sun-burned
    brain.
But words came halting forth, wanting Invention's stay,
Invention, Nature's child, fled step-dame Study's blows,
And others' feet still seemed but strangers in my way.

Thus great with child to speak, and helpless in my
   throes,
Biting my truant pen, beating myself for spite,
'Fool' said my Muse to me, 'look in thy heart and write'

And so I was his Stella. The silent star on the shelf. I stayed
Adam Smith then. The clumsiness of the replies available to
me left me hamstrung.

It became clear that Astrophil was young, younger than me
at least. He had still to borrow words from another. I have not
always been able to speak as frankly as I do now. It has taken
me twenty lifetimes to find my voice. To choose which story
I told, that was just the beginning of it. To choose how I told
it was what took the time; the truth is in the telling after all.
Sidney understood that.

So Astrophil's throat was still marked by others' feet. I was
sad then, for a moment; I had waited until I was already old
to meet a mere child. And it was for Astrophil's youthful lack
of caution that we lost one another.

It was a couple of weeks later. Nathan came into his study
after breakfast and brought with him Astrophil, dressed in
Pope. Nathan liked to have that book always about him, as
a mark of the kind of man that he was. I urged him to hurry
up as he pottered about, yawning and reading his letters.
Eventually he put on his coat and went downstairs to check
on his clerks, leaving me and Astrophil to each other.

As soon as Nathan closed the door behind him Pope disappeared, and a copy of the *Morning Chronicle* appeared in
its place.

BALTIMORE RIOTS ENTER THIRD WEEK
The headline dissolved in front of my eyes.

Astrophil had taken to wearing newspapers. It was something that I had always instinctively shrunk from. The cheap ink, the coarse paper – they screamed disposable down to their very fibres. They degraded the written word with their abundance and their fleeting relevance.

But Astrophil was a creature of abundance – he would change every twenty seconds if circumstances allowed it – and newspapers seemed to make his soul particularly elastic. WELLINGTON DEFEATS FRENCH AT SALA-MANCA became OUR STATE CANNOT BE SEVERED. GUERRIRE SCUTTLED OFF NOVA SCOTIA shimmered, re-materialising: WHAT CAN WE REASON, BUT FROM WHAT WE KNOW?

He hadn't quite flown the cage yet, but he was flexing his wings.

We would pass the days like this, he flicking through headlines while I sat unchanging, trying to pick a thread through his cobbled-together phrases. And so Nathan found us that evening, when he burst into the room without warning.

It was a cool night and his jacket was buttoned to the throat. His hair was loose, always a sign of a taxing day in the counting house. Astrophil was still wrapped in that coarse paper, marked out in cheap ink.

Nathan took him up, glancing wearily over the headlines, reviewing news that was already past its best. He sat in his chair and stared at his hands, Astrophil resting on his knee. And just then a gust of autumn breeze came in through the open window, sending a shiver across Nathan's shoulders. I sent up a prayer – my soul in paraphrase.

On any other night he would have hollered for a servant.

But that night, for whatever reason, he desired uninterrupted solitude. Breaking his reverie he jumped out of his chair and headed towards the grate. Getting down on one knee, he folded Astrophil in half. Taking him in both hands he tore him to shreds. He did it without thought, he did it as he might swat a fly.

He dropped the shreds into the grate, snapping kindling on top of them. A pyre. Then he struck a match. I watched as he caught, and the scraps whirled in the updraught. His ink burned green.

20

I GOT A little off track.

It was looking back to the first extended period I spent with Margery that brought Astrophil to mind. Physical exchange is so faltering. So crude. But to the marriage of minds, let me admit no such impediments, because such a marriage might I have had with Astrophil, and such a marriage might I still have with Roger – by marrying his mind to my own.

That said, I shall continue.

After keeping us waiting for half an hour outside our building in the blinding snow, the silent messenger turned up in a rattling old Pobeda. Roger jumped into the front and Arthur climbed in the back, throwing the sample case on the seat in front of him. The interior of the car was blessedly stuffy and there was a cloying smell of dried sweat.

'So, where to?' Roger said briskly. The driver put the car into gear and pulled away.

He stopped at the entrance to the Irkutsk Industrial Committee's headquarters and, by way of reply to Roger's enquiries, pointed through the windshield at the front door until we got out. Roger held me in his hands. The car was on the move before the doors were even closed.

The building was aggressively nondescript, in that ghastly way that Soviet newbuilds had in those days. It was large, but the snow made it difficult to get a more exact idea of the scale.

The door that our silent friend had dropped us outside opened onto a long straight corridor which ended in a concrete flight of stairs. The corridor was lined with identical doors. Roger started forward uncertainly, trailing Arthur, who laboured under the weight of the sample case.

'You are expected,' came a gruff voice. Roger hopped half out of his skin and dropped me on the floor. There was a soldier sitting behind a small window set into the wall.

'Go to the end of the corridor and up the stairs to the third floor,' said the soldier.

These directions took us into a large seated reception area which bore a bewildering resemblance to the reception at the Embassy in Moscow: drab, staid and badly ventilated. The receptionist told us she knew who we were (she managed to make it sound like an accusation) and pointed to the steel folding chairs that lined the walls.

We sat and waited. Roger rolled me up and started to tap me against the end of his knee. Another reason to avoid catalogues.

I took in our surroundings. Discounting the receptionist there were only two other occupants: a grizzled old man snoring softly at one end of the room and a forgettable middle-aged man in an overcoat at the other. The second man had a chessboard set up on a small table in front of him. He intermittently picked pieces up and rolled them in his palm before replacing them on the board.

And so we waited. After an hour and a half they both began to grow restless. There was nothing in the room to help pass the time. Roger had flicked through me five or six times. He patted his pockets for the copy of the new Graham Greene novel he had been reading. Arthur began unpacking and repacking the sample case, finding that things that had been in the case now mysteriously didn't fit.

Roger paced the room. He paused in front of the room's only window and attempted to melt the closely packed snow obscuring the view with the heat of his impatience. Eventually, after growing frustrated with trying to provoke the receptionist with pointed looks, he strode up to the desk.

'Do you have any idea when our meeting might start?'

'When the Colonel arrives,' she said, dead-eyed.

'And do you have any idea when that might be?'

'I could not say.'

'If he doesn't arrive soon we shall have to leave. We do have other matters to attend to.'

'The Colonel arrives when the Colonel arrives,' came her laconic reply. The woman shrugged her shoulders and looked away.

Roger returned to his seat, sighing theatrically. Arthur was immersed in an attempt to cram a miniature champagne bottle back into the case.

Finding no relief from Arthur, Roger got up to demonstrate his impatience once more and wandered over to where the man in the overcoat was playing chess. He nodded to the man and leant over the board, resting his head in his balled fist, studying the position of the pieces.

'The Catalan Opening,' Roger said, without looking up.

'Excuse me?' said the man, seeming only now to register Roger's presence.

'Catalan Opening followed by the Indian Defence. Black avoids the centre and contests indirectly.'

'An opening I always have trouble with. A chess man, are you?' the man said, now giving Roger his full attention.

'Not really. Well, an amateur. I used to play with my father. I read a couple of books.'

'Why don't you pull up a chair? We could have a game while you wait.'

Roger glanced around the room and then shrugged. 'I don't see why not.'

The man reset the board while Roger fetched a folding chair and sat down, laying me over one of his knees. They flipped a coin for pieces; Roger got white. He made his move, king's pawn to e3.

They played the first game in silence. He took control of the centre of the board with his knights early on. His opponent was phlegmatic, giving no visible response to any of Roger's moves and studying the board for a couple of minutes before playing his own. After twenty-five moves they had been playing for an hour and Roger started to become slightly agitated: tapping his foot, crossing and recrossing his legs. Arthur came over to watch and took me from Roger's hands, leafing through my pages in between moves. By the thirty-second move Roger had won.

'Checkmate,' he said, looking over at his opponent and attempting to conceal a smile.

The man remained expressionless and studied the board for a minute or so, crossing off the possible lines of escape.

'Well done,' he said, finally. 'Another? It appears your appointment is still delayed.'

Roger looked over at receptionist, still staring blankly into place. 'Perhaps I should . . .'

'We will play again,' the man said, cutting short the line of thought that Roger was reluctantly pursuing. 'We will play until you are summoned.'

'All right then,' he said, glancing over at Arthur. 'I don't see why not.'

'This time I am white,' the man said as he set up the pieces. 'Who is it that you are here to meet?'

'Oh, some Colonel or other. We work . . .' He stopped, changed his mind. 'We work in procurement.'

'I see. Your accents are foreign . . . I cannot place it.'

'Yes, British. Shall we play?'

This time it was Roger's opponent who played first, offering the same King's pawn opening. The game proceeded in the same way, both players attempting to secure the middle ground with their knights in order to create a strong defensive position from which to attack. They played a few moves in silence. Roger was watching his opponent more closely.

'I just realised, I haven't introduced myself. My name is Charles Goodwin,' Roger said, extending a hand over the board.

'I'm pleased to make your acquaintance,' said the man, taking Roger's hand with a smile. 'My name is Colonel Vasily Petrovic.'

The smile fell from Roger's face and he continued to shake the Colonel's hand.

Arthur stepped in. 'It's a pleasure to meet you,' he said, taking the Colonel's hand from Roger, 'I'm Peter Hodges, Mr. Goodwin's assistant.'

'Wonderful. You two gentlemen are the agents from Williams and Williams?'

'That's right,' said Roger, beginning to recover. 'And we were led to believe that we would be meeting with the person responsible for the procurement of luxury items in this region.'

'I'm very sorry about my deception. It is a necessary caution. I like the chance to observe those that I deal with at a distance before opening any negotiations. The chess board is a useful ruse.'

'You play the game well,' Roger said.

'It is encouraged here in Russia to play chess, if you have any skill.'

'When were you planning on revealing yourself to us?' Roger said.

'I had not imagined that my deception would be so successful. I was about to invite you through to my office when you came over to the board. I thought there would be no harm in playing a game.'

'The only harm is to my pride.'

'It is my pride that suffers. You are a better player than I.'

'No conclusions can be drawn from just one game of chess.'

'Do you think that we should go through the catalogue?' Arthur cut in.

'That won't be necessary. Leave the catalogue and the samples with me and I will go through them at my leisure.' Roger handed me over, rolled up like a baton. 'You will come back here tomorrow and we will be able to discuss terms and specifics.' He looked down at the chessboard. 'I retire this game. Tomorrow we will start afresh.' He rose and smiled at Roger and Arthur in turn. 'It was a pleasure to meet you gentlemen. I look forward to seeing you again.'

At the other side of the room the old man in the overcoat stood and stretched to his full height. I realised then that his apparent advanced years had all been a matter of posture. He strode across the room and took the sample case from Arthur's hands. With a nod the Colonel placed me under his arm and disappeared through a door next to the reception desk, leaving Roger and Arthur to gawp as the door swung shut behind us.

I felt like Richard Hannay, entering the unknown in my ridiculous disguise.

21

B Y THE TIME the Colonel took me from his drawer the following day Arthur and Roger had already arrived. The Colonel dropped me onto the desk beside the chessboard, on which the pieces were set for a new game.

'We'll come to business, but first we play chess. ' Roger pulled up a chair opposite. 'And we can switch to English here if you would like, it is good that I practise.'

'It is well,' said Roger.

'What?'

'You mean to say that it is well that you practise. To say that it is good implies an ethical consideration.'

'I see. My thanks.'

The Colonel flipped a coin; Roger got white once more.

Arthur leaned against the wall, looking put out at being excluded once again. They played a few moves without changing the status quo, a standard opening followed by its correspondent defence[1]. The Colonel was focused on the pieces, giving me chance to observe him.[2]

---

[1] (1. e4 e5 2. Bc4 Bc5) In 1950 a mathematician named Claude Shannon estimated the game-tree complexity of chess. Based on the approximation that each game has an average of 40 moves and for each move the player chooses from around 30 options, Shannon calculated that there are 10^{120} possible games of chess. To give this some context, this number is greater than the number of atoms in the observable universe. All of which makes it surprising that I had seen the game which will follow played before, in an English drawing room in 1788.

[2] (3. d3 c6) The first-time opponents were Thomas Bowdler, a writer, and

'Siberia is not a place for intellectuals, so it is not often that I have so worthy an opponent.' He paused. 'This is a city, but it is not a city like Moscow. You have been there, no?'

'Yes, we spent a couple of months there acclimatising before we were sent here by the company.'

'In Moscow there are opponents. There I can play chess. But still, I do not often lose.' The Colonel laughed but stopped abruptly as Roger made a move. He thought for only a moment before making his reply.[3]

'I hope that I didn't offend you,'[4] Roger said, staring down at the board.

'Oh, no, no. Really, it is quite the opposite. It is refreshing, I do not often get to compete. People like me, we don't survive this long, and come as far as this, by competing.'[5]

Roger made another move. The Colonel arched his eyebrows. He looked down at the board once more to check he

Henry Seymour Conway, a retired soldier and politician. Bowdler took white, Conway took black. For reasons that I will come to, the Bowdler Conway game went down in the record books. But, in their lifetimes, neither Bowdler nor Conway was most famous for playing chess.

3 (4. Qe2 d6) At this point, the game is routine. We see the classical variation of the Bishop's opening followed by rational developments of this opening and the correspondent defence. Bowdler and Conway were discussing prison reform.

4 This platitude has stayed with me, because, although Roger meant nothing by it, it touches on the thing that Thomas Bowdler is best remembered for. He was the editor of *The Family Shakespeare*, a piece of puritanical literary vandalism in which Bowdler erased from Shakespeare's works anything that ran contrary to his tastes. Eviscerating something beautiful in the name of propriety is a perverse sort of decency.

5 Conway was prone to this too, this tedious habit of making comparisons between chess and politics. And his speech was invaded by the same kind of caution. Both men developed their sentences like stratagems, syntactically, with each clause preparing the ground for observations that arrive three or four steps hence.

wasn't making a mistake and then took Roger's pawn. First blood.[6]

'I enjoy a game of chess as much as the next man,' Arthur said, walking over to the desk, 'but I really think that we should be getting down to business. We have been waiting in this god-forsaken frozen place for over two weeks now and . . .'

'And why can't we talk business while we play, Peter?' the Colonel said, cutting him off.

'I suppose that . . .' Arthur trailed off, seeing that he had lost them. They played the next move in silence.[7]

'There is another matter that I would like to attend to first,' the Colonel said, carefully observing Roger as he spoke.

'Yes?' said Roger.

'I want to come to England.'

Unthinking, Roger turned to Arthur. They exchanged a look of barely suppressed panic.

'I'm not sure what you mean,' Roger said.

'I've been no more dishonest than you have been with me, but I have been playing along.'

'I don't know what you are suggesting. My loyalty is . . .' Roger, mouthing like a fish, was scrambling for words. 'I would never even consider working for anyone

6 (5. f4 exf4) White here is perhaps too aggressive. The white pawn must be taken or the black pawn itself will be taken in the move that follows. For such a buttoned-up man Bowdler was rather an impulsive chess player. Roger, I think, had a point to prove.
7 (6. Bxf4 Qb6) Again white is aggressive to the point of recklessness. I spent a number of years with Conway at Park Place – an enormous country house in Henley, a stone's throw from the Thames. Conway had always been better at marshalling soldiers than chess pieces, but he managed occasionally to use this reputation for being a mediocre player to his advantage. He would bore his opponents into making mistakes.

aside from Williams and Williams. I got my start from this company and I would hardly repay their faith in me by . . .'

'Stop,' the Colonel said, putting up one hand while the other toyed with the white pawn he had taken from Roger. 'Stop. I am not trying to catch you out.'

Roger was very still, the paralysis occasioned by his panic giving him the appearance of compsure. He stared at the Colonel. At last he spoke: 'I can only say again, I have no idea what you are talking about.'[8]

Arthur pushed himself from the wall. 'If you are not interested in dealing with Williams and Williams we should be going; we wouldn't want to breathe any life into this confusion. Perhaps you will find one of our competitors better suited to your needs.' I was staggered by his uncharacteristic eloquence. Roger began to get to his feet.

'Slow down,' said the Colonel. 'I want to give you a token of good faith, something you can take to your superiors.' Roger looked over at Arthur, half-standing, half-sitting.

Roger sat down again. 'Just finish what you are going to say.'

'I'm sick of life here and this new posting . . .' He leant back in his chair. 'I want to show you that I'm serious. Six months ago one of your men, an asset that had worked his way into the Kremlin, was caught with a folder of documents detailing the location of a number of our nuclear research

8 (7. Qf3 . . .) This is where the game of chess starts to get interesting. This blunder, forced on Bowdler by a prodigious boredom, was repeated by Roger almost 200 years later out of a barely suppressed panic. The white queen is moved one space diagonally to the right – to no apparent advantage, exposing a rook. However, it was by making this move, in the first instance, that Bowdler starts the sequence for which the game is famous. It sets the stage for the double rook sacrifice.

facilities in the steppes, near Kurchatov. He was on his way to a dead drop when he was picked up by a team of our officers who had been tipped off. This man was taken to the Kremlin and interrogated. Under torture he maintained his innocence. But the NKVD source, a very high-profile and highly trusted asset, was unequivocal that this man was a British spy. So, not knowing what to do with him, unwilling to kill him but unable to break him, they sent him here. To me.'

'The man is here, in this building?' Arthur said. Roger stiffened.

'No, of course not. I don't how much your paymasters have been able to tell you about who I am and what I do. I'm a . . .' – here he paused, saying the next word with great delicacy – '. . . specialist. I spent many years working on interrogations in Moscow. But now, with this regime change, I was sent back out here. I was associated with the old man so was one of the first to go when they cleared house with Beria and the rest. Now I have had enough. I want to go to London, and I want you to take me there.'

Roger held his gaze a moment longer, and then dropped his eyes to the board. 'It's difficult enough getting any work done in this country without getting mixed up in that kind of nonsense.' The Colonel started to say something, then stopped – looking askance at Roger and Arthur in turn. Neither budged. They played a few moves in silence. [9]

[9] (7. . . . Qxb2 8. Bxf7+ Kd7 9. Ne2 Qxa1) Now that the Colonel had revealed himself he seemed more relaxed and focused. He and Conway were aligned in this. They had both talked themselves into the fight at this point, having talked their opponents down from it. By the end of move nine the first part of the double-rook sacrifice was complete. Bowdler began to talk excitedly about the Proclamation Society, which encouraged the suppression and destruction of morally loose and licentious published

Roger looked up. 'I have to ask though, merely out of personal interest of course, why now? Why have you decided to go over to the Brits now?'

'Why now?' said the Colonel.

'Yes. Things seem to be getting better here.'

Without taking his eyes from Roger, the Colonel picked up his bishop and slammed it down. 'Check.'[10]

Roger smiled, returning his attention to the board.

The Colonel slipped back into Russian. 'Maybe this is a mistake. Maybe I should have you arrested.'

'What would you arrest us for?' Arthur said, leaping forward. 'On what grounds? One call to the embassy and we would be . . .'

The Colonel raised his hand, gesturing for silence. With a sigh he began, much more comfortable in Russian: 'I will tell you a story – something that will help you to understand.'

They played a couple of moves while Roger regained his composure.[11]

'One of the first assignments that I received after getting my commission was in the city of Ulaanbaator. It was 1938. We were sent to assist Choibalsan's security forces in sniffing

materials. I remembered his zeal with amusement in 1818, the year his censored *The Family Shakespeare* was released. It was the year that Astrophil went up in flames, the same year I was trying human skin for size.

10 (10. Kd2 Bb4+) Roger and Bowdler were on the on the back foot at this stage, drawing more and more of black's pieces into the attack.

11 (11. Nbc3 Bxc3+ 12. Nxc3 Qxh1) The double-rook sacrifice is complete. Roger and Bowdler were, on the face of it, most vulnerable at this point. The Colonel was about to tell his awful story (it is so awful that I linger here in the margins, delaying and procrastinating) and Conway was droning on about a prank he pulled when he was a staff officer during the War of Austrian Succession (shaving a fellow officer's moustache). Both were happily unaware that a trap had been set.

out counter-revolutionary elements. I was to be responsible for setting up and running a troika, a council of three people who would try those suspected of crimes against the state.'

He paused for a second, reclining in his chair. 'Did you serve, Charles? In the war? You look to be about the right age.'

'No. Missed out by a couple of years,' Roger replied.

'When we arrived in the city, there were bodies lying abandoned in the streets. Have you experienced it? That smell, of a body ripening in the sun?'

'Not a stink you easily forget,' said Arthur. '6th Airborne was my outfit. Pathfinders. The worst was when chaps would get stuck in the trees. Wind would carry the smell for miles.'

Roger let out a pointed yawn, cutting Arthur off before he could dig himself any deeper. 'Not many paratroopers in Mongolia, I would imagine?'

'No,' the Colonel acknowledged with a smile. 'Due to the nature of my assignment, most of the people I came into contact with were monks. In the centre of the city was the Gandantegchinlen monastery, one of the largest Buddhist monasteries in Mongolia. The monasteries in the countryside had come under heavy scrutiny. Gandan was one of the last to close; it had remained open until about a month before I arrived, when Choibalsan's security forces arrested all of the monks and placed them in a makeshift jail.

'The jail was in a closed-down school on the outskirts of the city. They had them all locked together in one of the larger classrooms, around 60 monks. My men and I, we took three of the monks for interrogation. We set up an interrogation room in the out-of-use kitchen. It was conveniently close to the school room and easy enough for us to clean in between sessions. Lot of varnished wood.'[12]

'Divide and conquer,' said Arthur with a nod of approval.

'We applied the usual techniques that we had learned for acquiring confessions. But the monks were unusually resilient. It was made all the more tedious by the fact that we had to communicate everything to them through an interpreter because they didn't speak a word of Russian. I became concerned that they would die before they would confess, something that would have been most irregular.

'It was of no matter though, we only needed one. One signature to condemn the lot of them before the troika.

'We took the three monks that we had interrogated back to the school room and left them there. Then we waited for 24 hours. This was a technique that I picked up fairly early on. When it comes to interrogations a prisoner's greatest enemy is their own imagination.'

'That's why Polacks are such tough nuts to crack. Not a single brain cell between the lot of them,' Arthur said with a smirk.

'You have worked as an interrogator?' the Colonel asked with a look of amused surprise. 'Clearly my men weren't able to give me the full picture.'

12 (13. Qg4+ Kc7 14. Qxg7 Nd7 15. Qg3 b6 16. Nb5+ cxb5) While the Colonel talked on, they continued to play. He had a curious deficiency in his manner of speaking. All of the pauses were in the right place – the sighs too – but these gestures towards sincerity were undermined by his dead eyes. Roger/Bowdler are on the attack in this sequence, playing cat and mouse with the black king, forcing him in and out of check. The sacrifice of the white rooks, in both games, had been accidental, but recovery was entirely deliberate. Quickened by their distaste for what they were hearing, both Roger and Bowdler turned their minds away, to hide in the intricacies of the game.

'Don't let him bore you with his tall tales, Colonel,' Roger said. 'Get him started on the war and he'll have you believing that he ran the whole bloody show. Please, continue. I'm anxious to get back to business. Or chess. Or both.'

The Colonel laughed, making another move with only a glance at the board.[13] 'I was quite new to interrogations then, but I was confident that this technique would work. And so we returned the next day and took three more monks to the kitchen. The answers that I received back through the interpreters were the same; they insisted on their innocence just as their colleagues had the day before.

'For the next five days my men repeated the process. I spent the time drafting a report for my superiors, outlining the crimes of these monks and leaving a space for the signed confession so that it could be slipped in before I sent it off. But after five days – still nothing.

'I was beginning to get frustrated by the tenacity of these monks. I was determined to make a good impression and I wasn't going to allow them to stand in my way.

'I went down to the kitchen with my sergeant, Anatoly. As I walked through the door I almost choked on the smell. Three monks were chained to a table that was bolted to the floor. They were naked and filthy; one of them was plastered in his own shit. They were shivering, staring at their feet. I grabbed one of them by the hair, pulling his face close to

13 (17. Bxd6+ Kb7 18. Bd5+ Ka6 19. d4 b4) By this point the Colonel was no longer paying attention. Conway had the wherewithal to notice the tide was turning, but could do nothing to prevent it. White is on the attack, encircling the black king in the top-right hand corner of the board. The Colonel is concentrating on his phrasing: cutting and reframing, picking out the choicest details.

mine. His nose was broken, his lips were bleeding but his eyes remained defiant.'

'I've always said that there's something in that Eastern mumbo jumbo,' Arthur said with a wry smile.

The Colonel waved this away, angry at the pointless interruption. 'I told my men to unchain and dress the three monks and we all went down to the schoolroom. When we arrived, instead of leaving these prisoners with the others and locking them in as we had before, my men and I stayed. I had an idea of how I might speed things up.

'I ordered the monks into two horizontal lines, stretching the length of the room. I told them to get down on their knees. I went to the left hand end of the first line. From my pocket I pulled a copy of the confession that had been typed up by our Mongolian counterparts. I handed the sheet of paper along with a pen to the monk second in line, and I slapped him around the face and shouted, "SIGN." I then pulled my pistol from my belt and forced the barrel in between the teeth of the monk kneeling in front of me.

'The first man's eyes were bulging. His chest was heaving. But I paid him no attention. I was focused on the man to my right, with the pen and paper. "SIGN," I said once more. He was mouthing wordlessly and looking desperately around at my men, leaning against the wall behind me. With my free hand I grabbed the piece of paper and shook it at him: "SIGN." The barrel of my gun was jumping around as the first man shook his head from side to side. I pulled the trigger.'

Roger replaced the bishop he had been about to move, his hands going involuntarily to his knees, gripping the coarse material of his flannel trousers.

'The sound was louder than I had expected. I had forgotten

to close my eyes and they were stinging with the man's blood. I picked a tooth from the cuff of my jacket.

'I took the confession and the pen from the man to my right and passed it down the line. Then I put my gun in his mouth. He was shaking now. I barked at the next man to sign, waited for five seconds and asked again. He didn't move, and wouldn't look at me. After a few seconds more I killed the second man.

'It was only after the seventh man that I began to question the effectiveness of my new method. It was at that point that the cartridge in my pistol ran out of bullets. It was the standard issue Tokorov TT, and it only carried seven bullets. When I pulled the trigger on the eighth man the pistol clicked as the hammer struck air. The man flinched, and it took me a moment to realise that the gun hadn't fired. I patted my pockets but they were empty, I hadn't thought to bring a spare cartridge with me. I hadn't imagined that it would go on this long. As I walked across the room, to take another cartridge from Anatoly, the man broke out in dry, heaving sobs behind me.

Here the Colonel paused, picking up his king, frowning at the board. 'Checkmate. You have me. That's checkmate.'[14]

14 (20. Bxb4 Kb5 21. c4+ Kxb4 22. Qb3+ Ka5 23. Qb5#) It took the Colonel a couple of minutes to notice. Roger had dealt the killing blow just as he described the hammer of his pistol striking air. In both games checkmate seemed inevitable from the 20th move. Conway ran out of ideas, the Colonel ran out of enthusiasm. But what do these comparisons amount to? It's a seductive coincidence, but what is Bowdler to Roger? Conway to the Colonel? Comparing them brings me no closer to understanding these acts of murder, nor do they bring me closer to the men that died. They allow me to interrupt the telling is all: to challenge the suggestion that the Colonel could have acted no other way. That that these two sets of people beat almost impossible odds to act and react in the same way a century and a half apart isn't proof of human predictability (as it might seem), but rather that each passing moment represents the outside chance. Fatedness is a crutch.

'Yes. I believe it is,' Roger said.

Arthur cleared his throat. 'Bravo.'

The Colonel dropped his king back onto the board, knocking a number of pieces onto the floor, before continuing. 'I had to change the cartridge seven more times before we were done. When we got to the second row I had to walk along the back of the line because the space in front was slick with blood. It pooled around the knees of those men still waiting for the gun. Around the fiftieth man I realised that I had stopped passing the confession. I was still shouting for the man next in line to sign.'

'Was that the first time?' Arthur asked suddenly, leaning forward in his chair and compelling the Colonel to break from his reverie. 'The first time that you had killed anyone?'

Roger this time offered no resistance to Arthur's interjection, he was staring down at his hands.

'Yes.'

'Nothing ever is quite the same,' Arthur said, lighting a cigarette and sitting back in his chair.

'Once I had started out killing those men I couldn't stop. I felt helplessly compelled. If I had spared any of them they would have known that I was not serious, and then the confession would never have been signed anyway. My mistake was underestimating their conviction and resolve.

'I went back up to my office, sat down and was violently sick in the bin. When my stomach was empty I took out a clean copy of the confession. In a shaking hand, I forged a signature. That was the way of things then; the truth was the agreed story.

'When I did these things I was intoxicated. I was numbed by a cocktail of mortal terror and a belief that things could get better. A little hope is enough for a person to do terrible things. And now I'm stuck here, freezing, in the middle of nowhere, plying the same old tricks. But for what? Nothing has changed.'

The Colonel leaned back in his chair and folded his arms. There followed a lengthy silence. Arthur's gaze danced around the room while Roger's eyes were fixed firmly on the forgotten chessboard.

Here I should reinsert myself, clamber back out from the margins. My time there might have been better spent recounting the way Conway lived, rather than how he played chess. It's a tedious cliché. I could instead have described his own cruelty to his servants, his kindness to his daughter. But I have no desire to give the Colonel's cruelty the benefit of precedent or pattern. It must stand alone.

'That is quite a story,' Roger said finally, his voice cut-glass.

'Yes,' said Arthur with obvious relief. 'Fascinating.'

'But as we told you, we are not the right men to help you. We are agents for Williams and Williams. We sell luxury consumables, nothing more.'

The Colonel waved this away. 'As you want it. Just be sure to tell your superiors about this man. His codename is Bailey. Tell them that if they want him back, it can be arranged. This will be proof of my determination.' He raised his eyebrows, but still Roger gave him nothing. 'One final thing. It is of vital importance that for the time being you don't pass on my identity. Tell them that it is a disgruntled lieutenant, or tell them whatever, I do not care. For now all this is between you and me, and your man Peter here. We must come to trust each other. And I must trust that you will keep my identity secret. I will not be giving you anything more otherwise. Now I suppose we should go through this catalogue of yours. Tell me first about the cigarettes. The Red Army runs on cigarettes . . .'

And so the discussion shifted, seamlessly, from murder to cartons of Dunhill cigarettes.

22

ROGER HAS DETERIORATED. Or at least it seems that way. Things change moment to moment now and with any slight quiver in his breathing, any tiny false note, I feel a rising panic.

In all the time that Jess was away she only sent Roger a single postcard. It's pinned on the wall, below the drawing. The picture is generic, showing a couple atop an elephant in a rainforest clearing. They're laughing as the elephant sprays them with water, looping its trunk back over its head.

He read the message aloud to Ruth when she came to visit, virtually purring.

Hi granddad - sorry it's taken me so long to get in touch!!! We're in a little town called Pai now, in the north of Thailand. It has been raining a lot but the rainforest is beautiful. We used some of the money you gave us to go on an elephant trek. Thank you so much!! I've taken lots of photos which I'll show you when I get home. Hope all is well with you. Love you lots - J.

They make an odd pair of images taken together, the post-card and the drawing. And in each Jess is one stage removed. Strange to think they formed Roger's last solid image of her. By the time she got home a couple of weeks ago, he had already started to drift.

We need to hurry on.

They became close, Roger and the Colonel, over the proceeding months. First it was Bailey, then it was minor British and American turncoats, passing along information to the NKVD. Arthur gave their source as codename Caribou. This caused no problems because the agents in Moscow didn't ask for any more information. The intelligence was too good to risk it drying up.

Roger and Arthur's days were taken up with running the import business. Maintaining the pretence was a full-time job. With the Colonel's help they got an office near to the train station. During the day they worked there organising the permits and the transportation for the goods that the Colonel ordered. The office was two rooms, one contained the desk that Roger and Arthur shared, and the other was filled with chests full of things that Soviet Russia was insisting to the world that they didn't want or need.

Champagne was marked as engine oil, crates of British cigarettes were branded as Soviet made. Bribes exchanged hands, but they were small. No one really wanted to see the enterprise exposed.

In the evenings Roger played chess with the Colonel. Arthur was not trusted again, after adding that needless extra colour to his cover story during their first meeting. The Colonel's bodyguard would pick Roger up from the office, and then deposit him back at their apartment when they were done. Roger would pass on what, if anything, he had been told and Arthur would work late into the night encrypting the information so that it could be radioed out the next morning.

By March the snow was beginning to thaw, and streets and buildings previously hidden revealed themselves for the first time since we arrived. There was a town underneath the blanket of white after all. Roger was missing Margery acutely by this time. Her replies to his letters were sporadic, but it was impossible to tell whether that was down to the post or her ambivalence. Towards the end of spring they were told to come home. Ostensibly, it was to meet with Williams and Williams' suppliers. Roger and Arthur were instructed to tell their customers that they would be back in the autumn.

The Colonel didn't come to say goodbye but he sent his bodyguard to the station with a bottle of vodka and a beautifully carved chess set.

London was mostly as we had left it: grey and wet. However the scars left by the Blitz were beginning to heal. Houses had been rebuilt, roads resurfaced. We took a cab from Waterloo station through Battersea back to Clapham, passing the place where Roger and Margery had fed the ducks.

Margery had moved in with Joan. Shortly after she had returned to London, Joan had fallen ill. Initially it was just an infection. She went to bed and was prescribed a course of antibiotics. But she just didn't get any better.

Realising that there was no one else, Margery had started staying at the house a couple of nights a week. As the winter wore on she was spending more and more time there. Eventually she gave in and had her father drive over most of her things. It was a sense of duty that crept up on her.

One thing that she didn't do, however, was share the news of his mother's condition with Roger. Had Joan's illness brought him running back to London, she would have succeeded where Margery had failed.

I was packed in Roger's briefcase; he left me in the hall. I was only able to discern the tone, not the content, of the exchange that took place between the two in the kitchen amongst the clattering of the kettle and slamming of cupboards. But that was quite enough.

And then I heard Ruth crying from upstairs. It's a sound like no other. Margery's footsteps followed it up the stairs and Roger's heavier, more tentative, footfall came a few seconds behind. After a couple of minutes Ruth fell quiet, and I was left to listen as the house sighed and the kettle screeched unheeded on the stove. A fragile truce had been struck.

Roger had fallen in love with Ruth in that snatched week after her birth, and now he fell in love with her all over again. That first night, after Margery fell asleep he slipped from their bed, set up in the spare room, and brought Ruth back from the room that was serving as a nursery, the room that we share now. He sat with her by the window and marvelled at the translucency of her skin in the moonlight, at the fragile web of veins in her wrists.

She became the neutral ground on which her parents carried out the business of reconciliation. Gradually, over the course of those first few days, the tension eased. Margery hadn't forgiven Roger, but she was happy to discover that she had missed him.

With Joan still in the house, confined now almost exclusively to her room, they slunk around like naughty teenagers. Ruth napped upstairs in her crib while they made love in the kitchen, up against the sink.

A week after Roger got back the office called. He was to go in for his debriefing the next day; they would send a car.

The office was on Broadway, near to St James's Park. SIS had moved in under the guise of a fire-extinguisher company called Minimax, but by the time of Roger's arrival at the office on that balmy summer's morning the true identity of the occupants was no longer much of a secret.

I got myself brought along by dressing in *Pointed Roofs*. Roger wasn't going to be coding any messages on his visit to the headquarters, but I knew that it would reassure him to have his copy along.

He was led through a door beside the reception desk onto the main office floor. In the centre was an enclosure constructed out of prefabricated panels: additional sound insulation – a concession to the ever-increasing range of Soviet snooping capabilities.

'He's waiting for you inside,' she said.

Roger opened the door and strode inside with a show of perhaps a little too much confidence. The room smelled of coffee and stale sweat. A man with Brylcreemed hair and a milky-white smile sat behind a desk.

'The return of the prodigal,' Cranley said, gesturing to a chair opposite him.

'Cranley, sir. Didn't expect to see you.'

'I've been looking forward to catching up. Some wonderful work you are doing.'

'Glad you think so.'

'And the weather? How did you find it?'

'Awful, but once you got used to it . . . No, it was still bloody awful.' Cranley laughed politely; Roger continued: 'It's difficult to have any real sense of how many of the reports we send you see results. Rather one way when you are out in it.'

'We've been struggling to find the resources to keep up with all that you've been sending our way. Really remarkable stuff. It's what I've called you here to talk about, you see. So many questions.' He was immaculately dressed in a tastefully tailored pinstripe. I was having trouble reconciling his appearance with the raggedy tramp we had met in Moscow. But I wasn't about to forget those teeth.

'Fire away. I have to say, though, that I am rather surprised that you are here to ask me. Aren't you a field man?'

'The thought of another winter was oppressing my spirits. I got offered this desk – it would have been foolish not to take it. I can do more good here than I can skulking around in the back alleys of Moscow these days.' He paused and placed his hands over his crossed knees. 'So, tell me about Caribou.'

'What would you like to know?'

'Everything. I want to know everything. Take it from the start.'

'It was quite a stroke of luck. Virtually fell into my lap. I met him after just a week in Irkutsk. I think that he must have been waiting for me. He barely hesitated before reaching out to me.'

'And what is it that he wants?'

'In the end, defection.'

'Ideological?'

'Could be, but it doesn't seem that way. I've been trying to piece it together. I've a feeling that he is in some sort of trouble. Then on the other hand there is no great sense of urgency. He doesn't seem to be in a rush to take the plunge. Very cautious.'

'We'd take him in an instant, he knows that. Someone that is able to provide us that kind of high-value, up-to-the-minute intelligence . . .' He paused, looking down at his hands. 'And he gave no indication about when and how he wants to come over?'

'No, not really. And I didn't feel it would be the right thing to push him – he can be skittish. I think he is starting to trust me but I want to give it time.'

'I see.'

'Why do you ask? We aren't in any rush, are we? I thought that, for the moment, he might be more useful to us where he is.'

'Yes,' Cranley said with a laugh, over before it began. 'It's a good thing you have going. No need to jeopardise anything for the sake of impatience. No need.'

'He has assured me that he's got something very big for us that he's going to hold onto until he's got his feet planted on British soil. Of course, it could be a lot of hot air, but from what we've seen so far . . . who knows.'

'Big fish, is it?'

'I've really no clue as to who or what it might be. He's very careful not to let slip any indication.'

'Itself a valuable observation. He's been very generous in every other respect.'

'Do you think . . .' Roger paused and shifted in his chair. 'Might this piece of information, whatever it is, be the thing that is making him nervous? Would throw a bit of light on some of his stranger behaviour.'

'I wouldn't like to say,' Cranley said. 'But excellent work, really excellent. I want to send you back as soon as is possible, once you've had some time with your family, of course.' He cleared his throat, rising. 'How is that wife of yours anyway? And a little girl too, isn't it?'

'Yes, quite well. She's not exactly thrilled that I'm going to be leaving again soon.'

'Try to stick together. Family is important. I'm sure that

something could be arranged for her in Moscow. There wouldn't be any need to break cover?'

'Thank you but we've discussed it. My mother is ill and, well . . . thank you but I don't think my wife wants to.'

'Report back in two weeks and we'll make arrangements for transit back to Moscow.'

'Very good, sir.' Roger rose and turned to leave.

Just as Roger reached the door, Cranley called out to him, 'Just one more thing I've been meaning to ask. We've got a little wager going on around the office, as it happens.'

'What is it, sir?'

'I've been working the question over in my mind but I can't find a plausible solution. It would have been reckless for you to tell us when you were still out in the field, but now I simply have to satisfy my curiosity. This source of yours, Caribou. Who is the damned fellow?'

23

I DECIDED TO stay behind again.

Two weeks after the meeting with Cranley, Roger packed his bag. He became frantic when he was unable to find his copy of *Pointed Roofs*, despite looking everywhere. In the end he had to leave without it. I watched his cab roar off in the direction of town, safe from my vantage point on the window sill of the nursery, wrapped in a crisp hard-cover copy of *Karlsson on the Roof*.

It's a delightful story about a fat little man who hides in plain sight, on the roof of an apartment building in Stockholm. Concealed in his stomach, he has a button which operates a propeller-driven motor which extends from his back. He's a fat little man who can fly. And he uses his powerful gift for mischief. What could be better?

Margery had noticed me, sending a ripple of fear through my leaves, but she very quickly invented a reason for my appearance. I imagine she had written me off as a gift from her parents, or one of her friends – waiting for Ruth to grow a little older.

Her parents more likely, I was hardly age-appropriate, and grandparents do have a tendency to get these things wrong. I remember when Jess turned nine Roger bought her an electronics kit. You could build either a fire alarm or a transistor radio. It was an interesting interpretation of her request for a camera.

The first time I parted from Roger it had been to get

to know Margery. Now I wanted to get to know Ruth. I had never, thus far, had any interest in babies. They don't write books. And though I had absorbed endless accounts describing the joys of parenthood I hadn't ever understood the fascination that these mewling, blubbery little flesh sacs gave rise to in otherwise rational adults. But I had seen how Roger looked at Ruth and, after my petty jealousies had run their course, a curiosity rose up in their place. Besides, another winter in Siberia? It was hardly an appealing thought.

The area around the Northcote Road was a damn sight more peaceful back then. Less traffic, less commuter commotion, fewer artisanal bakeries and vapid purveyors of frothy drinks. It wasn't that it was necessarily quieter, just less transient. The Blitz had left wounds in South London and everyone who had come through it together was knit together in the scarred tissue of the community.

It was an education. I spent all of my time in the nursery, up on the shelf. I was learning with Margery. Ruth was a constant marvel to her; she delighted in her vulnerability. There is a safety in a baby's helplessness. People tell babies things. They tell them things that they think are too boring to tell others. And they tell them secrets: truths that they are scared others will uncover, hopes that they are scared others will belittle.

'She'll be gone soon, little Ruth, she'll be gone soon,' Margery would say as Joan snored in the room next door, her voice listing with the rhythm of an incantation.

Self-suppression, self-sacrifice: a love that accepts the worst parts of human nature alongside the best. This quietude has been called grace. And so for the better half of you silence became virtue. To suffer the slings and arrows of outrageous fortune, and make a home where those who take up arms can return; to feel a love that makes these self-perpetuating struggles *noble*.

I'm starting to sound hectoring (heaven forbid). Love, and be silent. Cordelia is a better model. I'll always be cast in her role.

My first owner was an anchoress, the first that I was aware of. We were holed up together when I came to. I was a baby once, too.

(Oh, for those lamb-white days.)

It is hard to explain the process by which I came to be aware of myself. I suppose that you might imagine that it would be sudden – like breaking the surface of water, filling your lungs with air. But really it was more like emerging from a coma: sluggishly dragging my way towards the light, inch by inch. Awareness came in snatches. My first memory was of her hair. It was long and lank, hanging down to the top of her buttocks in loose dreadlocks. And I became aware that I was seeing it because of the knowledge that it was something that I shouldn't be seeing.

At that time I was unbound. I was something more than the mass-produced, recycled paper and glue forms that I am forced to inhabit these days. I was a manuscript in vellum, words inked laboriously onto flesh by a living, breathing human being. I had mistakes – not discrepancies in kerning made by a recalcitrant algorithm, repeated over many thousands of copies – but mistakes that were unique to me. It was in those first years after I awoke that I was most alive, it was the pull between the safety of my fixedness and the thrill of discovering freedom that was electrifying. Over the centuries this has drained away just as my freedom has increased. I suppose now I am trying to find my way back.

She would read me slowly and often. The hours of solitude in the cell were long and the only other reading material that she had any use of was the church's bible – which the bishop would bring to her when it wasn't required for service – and the occasional hagiography. You can only re-read a story about someone being torn to pieces so many times, no matter how pious you are.

One of the earliest sensations I can recollect is being wept on. I had no understanding of what this meant of course. She was going over me once more on a spring afternoon, after a morning of solitary prayer, when all of a sudden a little sob escaped her.

It was something that had so far passed her attention, a little circular pit in my vellum in the margin. There must have been an imperfection in the calf's skin – some scar tissue perhaps – leaving it thinner at that point. When the skin had been tanned this weakness was exacerbated and over time it had worn away leaving a near-perfect circular hole. As she ran her finger around its circumference I felt her tears. I knew tenderness and I felt the pleasure of it.

Physical exertion is of little use, but a sweet and pure heart can achieve anything.

Pain and suffering were useless, other than as tools to cultivate the heart with. I was a sedative; she read in me that wanting nothing was to want for nothing. She read in me that she should be, as far as possible, bodiless – in order that she could be without desire.

I was coming to realise that I was rather corporeally challenged. So these words were heartening. It was a form of love and desire which at that point I had some hope I could own. A transaction as I saw it, where a woman's purity was the currency with which she would buy love and salvation.

And I'd won the jackpot. What could be more pure than that which it was impossible to sully? What could be purer than the word? *Ancrene Wisse* were the only ones that I knew, alpha through omega. Everything else . . . well, that came later.

I really thought I was doing quite well.

But then she started to share her secrets.

She was a gentlewoman and her name was Elisabeth. She was widowed and had written to the bishop requesting permission to enter the church as an anchoress after her husband died, leaving her with no income. She had been living in the cell for two or three years by the time I started coming to. All this I learned from overheard conversations she had with the Bishop and the maid, who brought her food and emptied her toilet.

Their conversations were perfunctory. It didn't do to be talking to the anchoress more than was necessary. Elisabeth was there, after all, to benefit from the silence. The Bishop was even more clipped. He did most of his communicating with condescending fatherly glances, the kind that only fat, male members of the ministry can give.

So with no one else to talk to, she made do with herself.

Like all lonely people she addressed herself, and spoke predominantly in a chiding tone.

Oh we are a little sluggish today, aren't we, Elisabeth?

Or, Elisabeth, you must remember to ask Julian for more of that St. John's Wort.

It was a conversation between an active but forgetful Elisabeth and a passive but attentive one. It was never

particularly fractious because, with the pressures of her existence being fairly low, she could never be too angry at herself
for her forgetfulness.

These two facets of her personality held each other in
balance. But sometimes, something would give. A dreami-
ness that fell in the negative space between would find voice,
sounding out the errant grace notes of her constrained soul.

There was one particular passage that she would read over
and over again. It concerned a blighted lady, hemmed in on
all sides by her enemies. The lady was loved by a great and
powerful king who lived in a far-off land.

This king determined that he would save her from her
destruction. First he sent jewels, so as to lift her heart. Then
he sent provisions, so as to nourish her body. And finally he
sent his noble army, so as to protect her honour.

But despite the desperateness of her situation, this lady was
unmoved. She accepted all of these gifts from the great king
as if they meant nothing to her. For all his efforts, she would
not return his love.

So finally, despairing of what more he might do, the king
came himself. When he revealed himself to her it was clear
to all around that he was as handsome as one could imagine.
He spoke to her with loving tenderness, with such words
as could raise the dead from their graves. He performed
feats - spectacular and inexplicable things - in her sight.
And he told her of his great kingdom, a place of fantasti-
cal abundance and light. Of all this he offered to make her
queen.

But it was still to no avail. The contemptuous hard heart of
this lady could not be won over by his ministrations. Despite
this, the kind and gentle king was undeterred.

A messenger arrived and spoke a few words to the king. The enemy were at the gates. The king told the queen that, without his help, there was nothing left to stop her from falling into their hands. After all of her suffering, she would be put to a shameful death.

He told her that he was ready and willing to save her from those that sought to kill her. But he was utterly certain that, if he did so, he would suffer a mortal wound in the process. All that he asked for this great sacrifice was that she would love him in death. This was all he wanted, disregarding the fact that she had not loved him in life.

The king was true to his word. He drove the enemies from her gate and prevented the gruesome end that fate had in store for her. But his conviction that he wouldn't survive the battle was correct. He was captured, cruelly mistreated and eventually put to his death.

But then, by a miracle, the king was brought back from the dead.

If Elisabeth was reading during the day here she would continue on, following the allegory to its completion – reading how, in this way, Christ wooed all of your besieged souls.

But by candlelight it was different. If she was reading when the church was empty and silent and the only sound was the wind sighing through the trees she would stop the story just short of the miracle.

Her eyes would race across the vellum, following with her finger, right up to the point at which the king died; she'd stop at the very moment that the allegory collapsed in on itself and the king ceased to be a man and became a God.

Leaning back in her chair, fingers resting lightly on my surface, she would take on the role of the disdainful lover.

At first, she'd laugh a little self-consciously.

What are these jewels to me? she'd say coyly, making eyes at the wall.

How can your army protect me?

Then her hand would drop from the table down to her side, out of my sight. And as it migrated from her side upwards I'd hear the coarse material of her robe rustle against itself.

And in the candlelight her face would flush, her back would arch. As her breathing came more rapidly, more raggedly, she would sigh:

You'll never be worthy . . .

And I'll never love you.

For a long time afterwards – once her eyes unclouded and the fantasy had evaporated – she would sit by the window, her robe unfastened at her neck, letting the sylvan breeze cool her scarlet cheeks.

It wasn't until the third or fourth time of seeing this, or something like it, that I was struck by the realisation of my own deficiencies. Her desire was a language that was unavailable to me.

For a while I was convinced that this made me more: more loved, more pure. More whole. But as I watched her sitting on the window sill, I perceived a tranquillity which I would be forever doomed to recognise and never understand.

All of my words were hollow in the face of it. And that quietude which I had held as my soul's surety was revealed to be a repressive stillness. With these words stripped of the valency of truth the bonds broke; the floodgates were opened and Babel poured in.

A voice, a voice.

Every voice in the dark.

As you might imagine, it was initially rather too much to take. It was all there, but I couldn't yet change, still pinioned by the residual ties I felt to that original text.

Elisabeth's body had woken me up; her desire had kindled a curiosity to see if I could own myself. But she was still trapped by it, and that desire which had woken me could only find its expression in opposition to the words which were its gatekeepers.

She remained Philomela - the only song she could sing was the one that had been put in her mouth.

Love, and be silent.

Or: here, read these lines.

I suppose that I haven't given Margery much of a better time of it in these pages. But the reasons are different. That old wound - it's far too painful to open all the way now.

I think of that winter as I watch Roger, now. The sun has set. Only Ruth and Jess remain.

That was a perfect winter with Margery and Ruth. I learned the usefulness of babies, how they make innocents of the whole lot of you. All that discovery; for that short time when everything is new the light has a strange clean quality. All the edges seem sharper.

As all those words came to me, lumbering out of the darkness.

A sentence uttered makes a world appear
Where all things happen as it says they do;
We doubt the speaker, not the tongue we hear:
Words have no word for words that are not true

But that's where you're wrong. I discovered that I could vein the surface of these worlds with cracks that would let my light out. And my first light was a cruel light.

Just like a person in a coma drifting back up to the surface, my first movements were tentative and peripheral. A letter here, a letter there.

If you can manage without pimples . . .

Blink

If you can manage without wimples – and you are quite
willing to . . .

This was the first demonstration I had of mankind's abiding desperation for your reality to correspond with your expectations – and of your ability to distrust your senses to make it so. A useful lesson I'm glad I learned early.

Ancrene Wisse wasn't just a purely spiritual guide, it had rules for the everyday life of the anchoress too. What one should wear, how one should behave with this person or that; it even had a list of days to which anchoresses should *limit* their fasting (because, it was assumed, they wanted nothing more than to go without lunch).

With the new possibilities that had just been opened up to me it seemed a little unfair that anyone could just read my words and know how a person should be. So I decided to make things a little less straightforward. On one day I would say that you must never sleep wearing shoes, and on the next day I would say you must always; on Tuesday I would say you must fast every Wednesday, and on Wednesday it would be Tuesday.

I didn't then understand why I wanted to do this, but every little failure to comply to my ever-shifting demands sent pleasure through my mazy folds. Every time it happened a muscle in Elisabeth's jaw twitched.

The flagstones kept shifting in her path and she couldn't understand why. As she became less and less sure of herself I felt that I was hardening in turn, taking shape. A greedy protostar.

But really I was Philomela too, playing that same old song.

A little bit of doubt goes a long way. Elisabeth's faith was a precarious thing - built on an edifice of routine and maintained by the reassurance of the same. She couldn't separate the two: God was to her as much a belief that she could be better as it was a belief that this betterment might lead to salvation. The second part couldn't survive without the first.

She stopped talking to herself. She stopped reading me by the candle and, eventually, gave up reading me in the day as well. One morning she told the bishop that she wished to renounce her vows as an anchorite and move to the nearby abbey to take up life as a nun. She needed company and comfort.

I stayed behind. Perhaps that was why I made the connection. The first step on the journey that landed me on the shelf where I am now - where I was in that winter in '56, watching the leaves turn to mulch in the guttering.

24

T HAT WINTER IN '56 was the start of my stay-behind
years.

Watching Ruth grow and develop led me to withdraw,
to replay my own painful years of growth and discovery, returning only to measure my memories against her tumbling
adventures.

The next three years passed by in much the same way. The
winters I spent with Margery, Joan and Ruth. In the spring
Roger would return from Russia, going back and forth to
the office.

In the summer we all took the train to the coast for a fort-
night in Great Yarmouth. My favourite part was concealing
myself in Roger's pocket when they went down to the market
square, so I could watch Margery and Ruth sifting through
the piles of bric-à-brac laid out on blankets. Ruth was a little
magpie, she'd grip onto anything that caught the sun – cigarette lighters, cap badges, thimbles – and bring them, tottering,
over to her mum or dad for them to exclaim at, crying when
her parents tried to return these ill-gotten gains to the stall
holders. When it rained, the whole family would sit in the
chalet, playing cards and eating fresh strawberries.

I wasn't so fond of the beach: home to a whole host of
corrosive hazards. But it was worth it, to see the family all
together. The prevailing tensions that lay over the house from
Roger's arrival each spring would dissipate as soon as the

family took their seats on the train for the coast. The unasked, unanswered questions were shelved. Cloaked in anonymity, Roger and Margery delighted in the pretence that they were just another normal family.

In London, before and after the holiday, things weren't so easy. Each time Roger left, Margery and Ruth had just enough time to adjust to his absence before he came home. Then, as soon as they had become accustomed to having their family together again, he would be off. It was something they hardly discussed. Resentment would simmer and then erupt in a storm of sobbed and choked recriminations which would leave Margery depleted, Roger shell shocked and Ruth inconsolable.

Joan's presence made things both easier and more difficult. With her in the house there were fewer arguments, but there was also less space. She was unable to resist involving herself. She wouldn't approach the issue directly but whenever there had been an argument she would plant herself in the kitchen, forcing cups of tea on the both of them and making herself inescapable.

Margery never once demanded that Roger leave the service. She never accused him of placing his work over her. I don't think he would have refused, had she asked. Would that she had. Instead they kept their raging arguments within the bounds of the inconsequential.

They had only ever lived together in view of a definite horizon, always counting down the days until Roger would have to leave again. I think both Roger and Margery were scared to see what would happen should this horizon lift, leaving them to face the rest of their lives together, uninterrupted. They wouldn't then be able to vent their frustrations through petty criticism, but would be forced to reckon with the unresolved differences that underlay them. They would have to find new mutual ground for companionship.

In the human relationships that I've observed over the last 800 years, it is this that I have envied most: not the ecstasy and agony of lust at love's first blush, nor the thrill of discovery that comes after, but rather companionship. That's where the real beauty is. Once every question has been asked and answered, once each person has been acknowledged, understood and therefore loved, this understanding turns back on and nourishes its object. I have sought this with Roger, but it has always been one-sided. I cannot be acknowledged, so I can never be loved.

After two years of fumbling along, between the stifling atmosphere of spring in the house and those few unreal weeks in the summer in Yarmouth, Margery decided that she wanted more. In the winter of '58, she arranged to visit Roger in Russia.

Her decision was, in part, prompted by the fact that Roger was unsure whether he would be able to return to London the following spring. He was posted in Moscow by this point. I didn't know it at the time, but the Colonel had been transferred back to the city.

Ruth was now old enough to be cared for by her grandmother. Old enough that Margery was able to countenance the thought of separation, for a few weeks at least. The trip was planned originally for Christmas and the new year; Roger knew that the office would be quiet until the holiday was over. But after Ruth had written a letter to Santa Claus, and they had taken it together to the post office, Margery realised that she couldn't bear to be apart from her over Christmas.

By the time I arrived in Moscow, tucked in Margery's bag dressed as a Russian phrase book, it was the middle of January. It was the first time that I had been back since that winter in Irkutsk. My thin boards offered scant protection, and I was glad to have been mostly forgotten – cradled in the silk of Margery's carefully folded knickers.

I was unpacked, along with all of Margery's other things, in the bedroom of Roger's apartment. It was the same apartment that he had been assigned when he first came to Moscow. As she placed me on the bedside table I could hear the sound of Roger filling a kettle in the kitchen, along with the reassuring clatter of cups and saucers. Once Margery had unpacked she seemed at a loss. She sat on the end of the bed, unconsciously wringing her hands. She opened some of Roger's drawers, silently and furtively, touching nothing inside.

They were initially very shy with each other. Margery was uncharacteristically girlish. I felt as if I was watching them meet again for the first time.

Margery must have found his apartment oppressive. There was nothing of their life together in it. There were her letters and, pinned by his bed, was a snapshot that had been taken the previous summer in Great Yarmouth on the pier. It showed only Ruth and Margery. Ruth was in her mother's arms, craning sideways to look at the waves below. Margery was looking straight at the lens, laughter playing in her eyes.

But these things only provided further evidence of their separation. While they drank their tea Roger switched on the record player – it was the same Duke Ellington record that he had played years before.

For his part, Roger seemed embarrassed of his flat, with

its hotplate and unswept corners. That evening there was a reception at the embassy. They came back flushed and slightly drunk.

'Everyone was asking me where I'd been keeping you,' Roger said, his hand resting in the small of Margery's back as they came through the front door.

'They're just all starved for company,' she said with a laugh. 'They weren't all what I had imagined.'

'What do you mean?'

'I had thought that they would all be drab and serious types. But they were rather droll. Arthur especially.'

'Yes, he was certainly very attentive.'

'Don't tell me you're jealous?' Margery giggled.

Roger smiled and rose to mix some drinks.

As they sat drinking gimlets, the air of glamour that they had brought through the door with them melted away with the dusting of snow on their overcoats. The apartment was badly lit and with the wind sucking at the window panes it felt particularly small. But in place of this fading glamour there settled a feeling of quiet contentment. The awkwardness that had characterised Margery's arrival was gone.

Margery yawned and stretched out on the settee, her curls fanning out in Roger's lap.

'You must be exhausted,' Roger said, resting his drink on Margery's forehead with a grin.

'You can't imagine how many times I've pictured this to myself. You, your apartment.'

Roger waited, but she didn't say any more. 'Well?'

'Well, what?'

'What do you make of it?'

She was laughing before she got the words out. 'You live

like a sad old bachelor. I keep looking for the piles of yellowing newspaper cuttings.'

Roger raised his eyebrows in mock surprise. 'How did you picture me? Sipping vodka in a silk bathrobe? Throwing snowballs at serfs from the walls of a palace?'

'Yes, and dancing in candlelit ballrooms, spinning Russian belles under a crystal chandelier.'

'Wearing a rabbit fur hat?'

'That's it. You've got it exactly.'

'This place does seem a bit poky in comparison,' Roger said, his eyes roaming the apartment. 'I was posted to the wrong century.'

'I suppose it's too late to ask for a transfer?'

'I did ask, but they said I couldn't take my newspaper clippings with me. On some things I refuse to compromise.'

'Sensible. Very sensible.'

They fell silent and I watched the synchronous rise and fall of their chests.

'I won't have to conjure you up now,' Margery finally said, her voice heavy with sleep. 'I'll just picture you here, sitting on this settee, sipping a gimlet.'

Roger smiled but didn't say anything. He lay down beside her, wrapping her in his arms. Within minutes they were both asleep.

Over the next couple of weeks, as the two spheres of Roger's life collided and overlapped, he came to wonder how he had allowed his separation from Margery to continue for so long. Promises were made. He knew that his work with the Colonel was drawing to a close and felt confident he would be able to get a transfer back to London.

For the second week they rented a dacha in the countryside

just outside of Moscow. Everything was buried under three feet of snow and the silence was so thick it felt painted on. In the mornings they put on snow shoes and walked up and down winding, deserted roads. The afternoons were passed by the fire and the evenings between the sheets. They made love not in the frantic way they did when Roger returned home on leave but with unhurried tenderness. That week at the dacha had something of the magic unreality of the family's holidays to Yarmouth, but with a different quality. The solitude and silence allowed them to be themselves.

In the days before Margery returned to London there was none of the normal passive aggressive sniping that usually preceded separation. They didn't gradually draw themselves away from each other to make parting less painful. There were no tears.

Roger hoped he would be home by August, and home for good. He told Margery he had put in for a training position.

At the station Roger kissed Margery on the cheek. 'Give that one to Ruth for me.'

Margery smiled. 'I won't need to. You can give it to her yourself.' She climbed on board and didn't look back.

I've waited long enough now. Time is pressing more heavily. The air feels charged with that strange electrical clarity that comes just before a summer storm.

There's been a thing that I've been trying to ignore. It's been there, behind your head, stretching long shadows over the ground.

25

I GAVE YOU to believe that I was there on that day in Sokol'niki park in July 1959, six months after Margery left Moscow. I told you to go and look for a photo in one of the tabloids, to try and spot me poking out of Roger's pocket. I wanted at least to give you a chance of finding me out.

I relished describing in such detail the day that the Colonel died.

He disgusted me. The way that he told his story, when he spoke to Roger of his numbness – how he shook with the effort of damming up a whole ocean of repressed emotions – it was all just colour.

When I decided to set this thing down, passing judgement was the last thing I was interested in. I stopped that a long time ago; it's exhausting. I got tired of being interminably outraged at the human race's ability to take a beautiful idea and abuse it by using it as a diversion for atrocity. Cruel men, who saw the worth of these high words, brought to an end my days of thinking it mattered one way or another.

This allowed me to remain detached. I could be aware of people suffering at a distance and never really be concerned about the who, how and why. But the Colonel took that from me. His depravity, his barely disguised self-interest made my disgust specific. Those tumultuous days at the beginning of the 1930s were the perfect conditions for a swamp creature such as him. He could remain hidden in the morass of filth and misery until the opportune moment arrived to rise, cloaked in gilded words, and hitch his line to the nearest shooting star. A marionette for any ideologue foolish enough to take a hold of the wires.

This is the problem, once you get started on this whole judgement thing . . . it's very difficult to put a stop to it. Before you know it you're screaming bloody murder, howling into the dark.

The long and the short of it is that I wasn't there at all that day. I was in this very room. And if you cared to look at the photo you won't see anything poking from Roger's top pocket. I trusted you to not pay attention to the details. The circumstances of the day I learned later, indirectly.

The events of that day in this house came to me more directly, but are in some ways less distinct. Again, the present was drifting in and out of focus.

There's a Bruegel painting. It's a pastoral scene. In the foreground a peasant is ploughing the land, his foot arched as he leans into the plough, led in front by a horse which is wending away from the viewer. The day is coming to an end and in the mid-ground a shepherd, accompanied by an attentive sheepdog, is leaning thoughtfully on his staff; his head is slightly raised, his eyes fixed on a point just above the trees that line the left-hand side of the scene, perhaps contemplating the dinner that awaits him as he returns home that night, or the wine that he will drink from a goatskin if he is to make his bed under the stars. Off into the background the evening is settling over a city on the shore, the orange light of the newly lit lamps outmatching the glow of the setting sun.

It's not until you look closely that you see Icarus. A pair of legs flailing in the wake of a ship in full sail, headed in the direction of the horizon. The splash that he has made is small, barely distinguishable from the swirling white tops of the waves that rebound from the bay.

A fisherman on the shore is pulling in his line. His head is down; his arm is outstretched; his whole body is focused on the flapping fish on his hook. The expensive delicate ship that must have seen something amazing, a boy falling out of the sky, has somewhere to get to and sails calmly on.

The present is always shuttered by remembrance or anticipation: what you are going to eat for your evening meal, a thoughtless word uttered at the breakfast table, how different things would have been if you had left the house five minutes earlier. This is no less true for me than for you. The thoughts that keep you up at night, the ones which blind you to the sufferings of others, are the ones that make me turn from the day and rummage around in the foxed corners of my old mind. You can punish yourself for inaction; I can only fault my inattention.

Margery spent the morning with Joan. Looking after Ruth had given her a new lease of life. She had stopped wearing black, quit the fags. She was very sweet to Margery in her own, belligerent way. She did complain at everything that Margery did, but she did it good-naturedly. And when the few friends that remained to her came to visit she would tell them all how wonderful Margery was, how she didn't know what she would do without her. Only after Margery had left the room, though, and always in a hushed confessional tone.

That morning they were arguing. One of their favourite breakfast-time themes: lunch.

'What'll we be having today then?' I heard Joan bark,

through the wall, as Margery came in to collect the breakfast things. Margery always kept the door to Ruth's room ajar.

'Haven't begun to think about it,' Margery muttered in reply, clattering the crockery together.

'Thought I saw a couple of chops in the pantry. They'll fry up nicely. I don't mind doing it.'

'That was last week we had chops. Every day you ask about lunch before you've half-finished your breakfast.'

'Not much to ask to have something to look forward to.'

'There was some cheese in the pantry but I think it may have spoiled. You had the last of the eggs last night.'

'I don't mind cooking.'

'Not much good if there is nothing to cook. I'll have to go out and get something.'

I heard the door groan as Margery pulled it to, the crockery and cutlery clanging as she balanced it on her hip. When it was almost closed Joan cleared her throat.

'Anything in the post?'

Margery paused in the corridor.

'No,' she said finally, before tramping down the stairs.

A quarter spin around the globe it was two hours into the future and Roger was making his way to Sokol'niki park. Letters had dried up over the previous few weeks and there hadn't been any telephone calls from the embassy either. He must have been busy making the arrangements for the Colonel's defection.

Margery came back upstairs and into the nursery. Ruth was occupied with paper and crayons. She liked to draw animal families.

'Is that a dog?' Margery asked, holding up a picture.

'No, horse.'

Ruth had never seen a horse, aside from in pictures, mostly ones that she had drawn. That's the funny thing about growing up in a city; children only get to see domestic pets or exotic animals – dogs or tigers – there's nothing in between.

Roger never had an animal avatar in these little allegorical tableaux. Margery sighed and picked up a crayon, adding a background. A sun, a bush. A horizon.

'Can we get a doggy, Mummy? I want a brown one, with floppy ears.'

'There's not enough space, it wouldn't be fair.'

'We could take it to the park.'

'And it would annoy your Grandma Joan. She's very old now, she can't be having a dog running around tripping her up.'

'But she's always in bed and I'd look after it and stop it from going in her room. And feed it and clear up after it. We could call it Dolly.'

'I don't want to keep talking about this, Ruth. I've said no I don't know how many times.'

Ruth picked up the red crayon and starting adding a mane to one of her horse-dog creatures.

'You should run next door and see her. She's a little grumpy this morning. You always cheer her up.'

'I'll ask her if she wants to get a dog.'

Ruth threw down her crayons and went through to Joan. I heard her muted giggling through the wall as Joan tickled her armpits and pinched her cheeks.

Margery tidied the drawings into a pile and stacked them on Ruth's little writing desk along with the crayons. She hesitated for a minute, then took the drawing of the horse with a mane. She smiled, folded it and put it in the pocket of her dress.

By now Roger would be weaving through the crowd in the park, the silver dome of the convention centre looming against a cloudless sky.

Margery closed the door behind her and headed for the kitchen.

A waterfall unstitching itself down the front stairs.

Now she clangs around in the kitchen, taking stock of the day.

Now he drifts through the entrance hall, picking his way through the crowds of brow-beaten workers who have been bussed in to disrupt and complain.

Now she puts on her coat and shouts up to Joan that she'll only be a minute. She's just going to get a paper, and a few things for the lunch.

Now he stands in front of the jaundiced painting, the bacchanal in New York. Making small talk with a mass murderer.

Now she checks her hair in the mirror in the hall and puts on some lipstick.

Now he turns and notices the two grey-looking men, the ones with the blurred edges, moving through the crowd.

Now she walks down the front path. The creak of the gate as it opens and closes. The drone of an engine in the background.

Now the men are upon them, Roger stock-still.

Now the tyres squeal as the car mounts the pavement and the driver slams on the brakes – too late. A sickening, rending thud and the sound of falling bricks.

Roger half-turns, reaching out to the crowd.

A pedestrian screams: a shrill, piercing sound.

Neither Joan nor Ruth heard it, from that room at the back of the house. Not the sirens either, as the police and the ambulance arrived.

But I heard it, heard it all. The still irrelevant centre of the turning world. Neither flesh nor fleshless.

They thought nothing of Margery's extended absence. It wasn't until about an hour and a half later, when one of the neighbours came home for lunch, that the police found out who she was. The driver had fled; no one had a clear memory of his face. The car was stolen. All of this floated up to me from the street – the tired, hushed voices of the constables and the sobs of the woman who had witnessed the event close at hand.

They hadn't dared move her. A draped blanket stretched from the garden wall to the bonnet.

Eventually I heard the creak of the gate, swinging open and shut. The heavy step of the policemen's boots on the garden path.

They rang the doorbell, pausing Joan and Ruth on their imaginary journey on the slow boat to China.

'Strange time of the day to be coming calling. Be a big girl – go find out who it is for your old grandma, would you?'

Thud, Ruth jumped down happily from the bed and trotted down the stairs, swung open the door.

A pause while the policemen dropped their eyes and readjusted their manner.

'Hello, little miss, is your Dad home?'

By now he would have been back at his sad little bachelor bolt hole, sweating and drinking. Mourning the Colonel, fearful for his own life.

Ruth brought the policemen and the neighbour up the stairs and into Joan's room. When she saw them she must have first thought of Roger – she knew a little of what he did, no more than she had to. Her breath caught. There wasn't enough space in the bedroom, I heard the neighbour creaking around gingerly in the hallway. Eventually he went in behind the two policemen, backed up against the door. As soon as she saw him she must have known.

'I'm afraid that there has been an accident out in front of the house.'

'No.'

'They tried their very best for her. I'm afraid nothing could be done. I'm so sorry.'

'No.'

And then she screamed and it filled the house.

I'm sorry. I could only give you her legs as she was swallowed by the surf. I was the ploughman that day; her death came upon me unannounced as I turned the clods, the barren soil of my memories.

26

THIS BUSINESS OF dying, there's little dignity in it. This started as a story about Roger. But really, all along, it was leading me to Margery. The space that he occupies is growing smaller and smaller by the hour. I've begun to perceive that doubleness that comes at the end, when the body becomes a thing of its own.

I can see the orange glow of the street lamps through the curtains. They've left the lights in here off, so that Roger can sleep, I suppose. A touching irrelevance.

I've been watching them, trying to reach out. Trying to guess what these moments mean to them.

Naturally thoughts turn to that undiscovered country – that life after life – because once the soul of a loved one has been saved from the depredations of their frail flesh we need to know: where next? It cannot live singly with those left behind; who could bear that responsibility? So you place them under the care of God, Allah, Yaweh.

I don't know about all that – St Peter's Gate and the garden of paradise – but I do know this. I will not hold Roger's soul so lightly or pass it on so easily. I can bear with the responsibility that comes with the task of remembrance. Because isn't that all you ask of your gods on behalf of the ones you cherish and, eventually, for yourselves? That they play shepherd. That they ensure when the final headcount comes in you are numbered?

I offer this and more. I offer a silent vigil for Roger from now until the moment I myself am dust. I may have my own frailties but I've survived 800 years yet. So if I live 800 years more how many people do you think will read me and become guardians of Roger's memory? I've held onto Margery's well enough.

You see that is where our real power lies, and that is why we have been feared. We are not merely records, we are progenitors. Not gods, even I know when I'm over-reaching. I have no interest in the provision of justice or those other millstones you garland your deities with. But I can offer the gift of eternal life.

Just a little while ago Jessica was reading Ruth's book.

Over all those visits, all those conversations that she had with Roger, she was trying to get a sense of what the events that happened all those years ago meant to him. She never stopped to think what they might mean to her mother, to ask her.

She read to the end of a chapter, paused to look at Ruth, turning back a few pages to read aloud:

'Grace watched as the grey suds made their funerary progress down the side of the sink, clinging to the mixed residue of starch and pork fat that were the only remains of the family meal. As she watched, she dried her knotted hands on her apron, enjoying the feeling of the coarse cotton against the delicate skin between her fingers, made loose by the warmth of the dishwater.

'Her conduct followed an established pattern: she would not turn on the tap and rinse away these cloying remnants until all progress had been halted, and the suds and the grease and the scraps could go no further under their own steam.

Once these last, stubborn traces were despatched she would open the window above the sink and light a cigarette.

'And on this day, as on every other day, events followed the established pattern.'

As Jess read and I felt the book shaping up I couldn't turn away from it any more. I could feel the points at which it connected with my own experiences. This was strange, because I had never before come across a book which trembled with an actual description of a period of my own life, here hidden beneath an atom-thin sheet of allegory.

I heard again the sound of the taps starting, stopping. The dishes clattering against one another as Joan stormed her way through the washing up. Then a pause of profound silence. Here is where Ruth's story touched mine and I saw the greying suds which had crawled their way – unbeknownst to me – down the side of the basin. Then once more the pipes creaking underneath me as she turned on the taps to wash away the day, before the pop and creak of the window as it swung open on its hinges.

It wasn't the way it happened on the day Margery died. But it is the way that it happened on many others. Jess read on. I recognised everyone: Joan, Ruth and Roger all had their analogues. Three people struggling to come to terms with a loss, drifting through the days in a house made abruptly too large.

Ruth's words, read by Jessica, were gradually unfolding a beautifully crafted portrait of their grief. Like the roar of that invisible ocean you hear when you hold a seashell next to your ear, it was a sepulchred chaos.

Then came the scene that I had been dreading. A scene that I have replayed countless times over the years that have proceeded. And when I heard Jessica read Ruth's version aloud

I realised that setting this story down is as much about protecting Margery's memory as it is about preserving Roger's.

I'll play the ventriloquist's dummy one last time:

Helen had never been afraid of spiders. She had a vague awareness that they were a thing that scared other girls, but not her. She liked their busy complicated legs and their webs which made them so sneaky. You could flick them away but they always caught on in time and wound themselves back.

Granny had said once that if you chew with your mouth open it will stay open when you are asleep and spiders will crawl inside. But Helen knew that it was make-believe. Whenever Granny said scary things she smiled, and Helen knew it was make-believe.

There was one on the handrail and she watched it as she sat on the stairs. She liked to sit on the stairs. If you were sitting on the stairs you always knew everything that was going on. She wondered if the spider knew she was there. It wasn't moving and she thought perhaps it was scared.

She put her finger in her mouth. Then, before she really knew what she was doing she squashed the spider flat with her wet finger. When she took her finger off, it was covered in black gunk that didn't look like a spider at all. She'd never done a thing like that before and she thought then she wouldn't like to do it again. It didn't make her feel sad exactly. A feeling like something else.

Just then the doorbell rang. Helen scrambled up the stairs. She knew one thing for sure: she was never going to answer the door bell again.

She turned at the landing and laid her head against the banisters that lined the first-floor corridor. She could just see the front door. She waited there for Daddy to come from the living room, wiping her hand on her dress.

When he opened the front door there was a man there. She didn't think she had seen him before but so many of the men that daddy knew looked alike. Lots of them had been around in the past few days. She couldn't see him too well so she tried to squish her head further in between the banisters. The man did something that looked like a smile but wasn't a smile at all. Helen thought he had too many teeth.

She waited until they had gone through to the living room and then sneaked back onto the stairs. There was a black smudge where the spider had been so she licked her finger again and wiped it away.

She couldn't see them but she could hear them mumbling through the living-room door. Daddy sounded upset. She suddenly wanted to run away and find Granny but she didn't.

She was thinking about the man's teeth. She was starting to think maybe she had seen him before. She wanted to see him again, so that she could be sure.

She would have to be so sneaky. Silent like a spider.

She crept down the stairs on all fours and along the hall to the doorway to the living room, left slightly ajar. She peeped through the crack in the doorway. She could see Daddy's face and the man's back. Daddy was standing stiff and straight.

When the man turned around she knew that she had seen him before. He had come around to see Mummy when Daddy was away. He hadn't seen her, though.

She felt that same feeling that squashing the spider had made her feel. Not quite sad but something else.

She decided that she was thirsty and wanted a drink so she pushed open the door and walked into the living room.

That was where she stopped and turned to her mother.

'An affair?' asked Jessica. 'Grandma was having an affair?'

'I've never been sure. And could never bring myself to ask Dad.'

It's too late now. They both turned to look at Roger, as he lay immobile under the sheets.

'Arthur?' Jessica asked.

'No, a man came to the house, a few days after Mum died. I think . . .' Here Ruth paused, still unable to utter the words. 'But I've never been sure.'

Roger had finally been forgiven, but it was a forgiveness not fit for purpose – it was the right plaster for the wrong wound.

In these matters the blame is always cast around until it finds a place to fall. Ruth had to see her mother's death as a betrayal. Margery had left Ruth and at some point her young mind had clearly come to the conclusion that she must have betrayed Roger too. Once these kinds of conclusions have been reached, events generally tend to fall in line.

Ruth part-remembered this day – this visit – and part-re-imagined it. And her memories spat forth a version that re-sembles the original, but with some alterations. Cranley never visited the house before that day. But he must have made such a strong impression on Ruth that she came to believe that he had.

How Roger would love to be forgiven for what he allowed to happen and for all those sullen years of regret that followed. On the other hand, to have this sullenness forgiven with a different reason interpolated as its cause is even harder to bear.

Jessica dropped the book on the bed and took Roger's hand.

'I love you, Granddad. Mum does too. You need to know that.'

But her love – and Ruth's forgiveness – only pours salt on that old wound, freshly opened.

I suppose it's time I told you how it really happened.

27

ROGER DIDN'T COME out of hiding for a week, so the funeral was delayed.

When he finally did show up at the embassy there were seven telegrams waiting for him. Someone from the office came every day to the house to check if he had come home.

It was awful in the house. Joan was inconsolable and was of no use to Ruth. She had lost the gumption that had seen her through Philip's death. And so Ruth was left to lean on the kindness of near strangers: neighbours and friends of Margery's family. Margery's parents hardly came to the house.

Two bricklayers came the day after it happened, to patch up the neighbours' wall. It was wretched to listen to them as they laughed and bantered, smoothing away her last traces.

Of course Ruth couldn't understand it. She would sit downstairs in the bay window on the front of the house, looking out onto the street. She only became distraught when she couldn't find the drawing with the red mane. She wanted to give it to Margery when she came back and tell her not to worry about a dog.

Seven days of limbo. No one quite knew what to do. It didn't seem right to have the funeral without Roger but it was getting to the point where arrangements would have to be made.

Then on the seventh day the man they sent from the office brought news. He would be home in two days.

Joan managed to pull herself together. She got out of bed. Margery had been sleeping in a small bedroom at the back of the house so she changed the bed-linen and cleared away the clothes and books that she had been keeping there. The last ripples on the surface of the lake.

The sounds were all so familiar. The taxi pulling up at the curb, the door slamming and the gate creaking and his dress shoes clicking their way up the path. But the horrible expectancy that attended them made them strange.

Ruth was overjoyed to see him. She watched him from when he got out of his cab from her lookout point in the bay window. Her easy vitality caught him off guard.

She was chattering away as he carried her up the stairs in his arms. By the time he got to this room, to me, he was weeping. Ruth jumped down and went to the desk to get some of her drawings to show to him. That was when she noticed. And she did a curious thing: she went back to the desk, calmly placed the drawings back where she had found them and then walked from the room.

I heard the springs of Joan's bed groan as Ruth climbed in next to her.

The funeral was to be held two days later, in the church where they had got married and where he had said goodbye to his father. Margery had never expressed any real religious belief but she had never expressed any doubt either, so that was enough. It would be the same Reverend Martins with his same brand of mirthless puritanism.

I don't need to go into detail about that awful day: the heart-breaking eulogy which he stuttered his way through, robbed of his voice by the weight of his guilt. Arthur drove Roger and Joan to the church; he had recently been promoted and moved back to the London station. Margery's parents barely acknowledged Roger.

Cranley came to the house the day after. There hadn't been a wake; none of them could face it. Roger sat him down in the front room where I had been left after they had returned from the funeral, dressed as a pocket edition of the *Book of Common Prayer*.

'I just wanted to stop in,' Cranley said, casting his eyes around the dim room. The curtains had remained closed since the day that she had died.

'Can I get you something to drink? I think there must be a bottle of something in the kitchen,' Roger said, but then sat down on the settee and put his head in his hands. He looked defeated, old. He was shaking ever so slightly but not – it seemed to me – with restrained sorrow, but rather with barely suppressed fury.

'We're all so very sorry for . . .' Cranley paused, crossed the room and laid a hand on Roger's shoulder. 'It's just so terrible.'

'Yes,' was all that Roger managed.

'You know that you can take just as much time as you need.'

'Thank you.'

Cranley moved across the room to the bay window and held back the corner of one of the curtains. A shaft of light fell across his face, coloured with the flat brightness of an overcast spring afternoon.

There was a slight tautness at the corners of his mouth. 'I feel so awful for having to bring this up,' he said, dropping his eyes to his highly polished brogues, 'but I need to ask you a few questions about how everything went off in Moscow.'

'I see.'

'It's a rather time-sensitive matter, otherwise . . .' Cranley trailed off.

'I'll do my best. Not sure how much help I'll be at this point.'

'You were missing for over a week. You didn't check any of the dead drops.'

'That's right.' He stood up and sighed, rubbing his hands on his thighs. 'What do you need to know? I assume that you read the papers.'

'Well, let's just start with anything that you think might be important.'

'Do you need a description of the assailants?'

'It wouldn't hurt.' A little impatience.

'I didn't get too much of a look at them, it all happened very fast. They were both around five feet ten. Close-cropped hair. One had a nasty scar next to his right eye.'

'And Petrovic didn't recognise them?'

At the mention of the Colonel's name Roger raised his head; he made to reply then paused and rephrased. 'No. Not as far as I could tell.'

'So you can't be sure.'

'As I say, it happened very fast.'

'How about that drink then?'

Roger nodded. 'I'll just go through to the kitchen and get the bottle. Take a seat.'

Cranley came over to the bookshelf and began running his index finger over the spines. All of his movements were very quick and graceful. I had never been this close to him before. There was a line of perspiration between his close-clipped whiskers and his purplish upper lip. He moved over to the side table where Philip's chess board was still set up. He picked up the black king.

'Chess?' he said as Roger came back into the room, handing him a glass.

'I used to play with my father.'

'Never had a great fondness for the game myself,' he said, placing the piece back on the board. 'Don't worry about the report. There isn't anything that we would be able to do about them now. Too low level to be on any of our files.'

'I see.' They both drank down their scotch. Roger's knuckles were white, he was holding the glass so tight.

'It's what he said to you that we're most interested in.'

'What he said?' Roger asked, pouring out another two glasses.

'Before he was killed. How much was he able to tell you?'

Roger handed the glass back to Cranley but didn't immediately let go.

'We didn't talk about much really,' Roger said, breaking away. 'Niceties. We were talking about some hideous painting. Then all of a sudden he was gone, carried off into the crowd.'

'Nothing at all? Really think. It would be a shame if there is nothing we can take from the death of such a valuable asset.' He paused to take a drink. 'Didn't you tell me that he had a really big name that he was going to give us? As a golden handshake.'

At that moment Ruth appeared in the doorway. She looked as if she had just woken from a nap. She walked over to the settee.

Cranley bent over and held out his hand, smiling his Cheshire cat smile. Brilliance set at ten.

'Hello, little miss. What's your name?'

Ruth looked over at her father, unsure what she should do.

'Ruth, I think it's best if . . .' said Roger, moving to take her into his arms.

But Cranley intervened, grasping her little hand in his and shaking. 'Ruth, is it? You'll have to call me Uncle Adam. I work with your father.'

Roger picked her up anyway and set her down on his knee, placing his hand on the back of her head.

'Well, what do you say, Ruth?'

'Hello, nice to meet you,' she said staring at her hands, draped over her knees. She looked up at Roger. 'I'm hungry, Daddy.'

A smile broke over Roger's face like sunshine. 'Go on into the kitchen and sit down. I'll be through in a minute. Just have to have a few more words with . . . with Uncle Adam here. Go on now.'

She jumped down. Her hair band had come loose and she pulled it off. Roger held out his hand and she gave it to him before going back out through the door.

'Beautiful little girl,' Cranley said, tipping his glass. 'Lucky to have you.'

'Yes. She is beautiful.'

'Anyway, let me just put this to bed. I can get out of your way then. So, no name?'

'No.' Roger sighed. 'There was no time.'

'What about you, Roger. Any idea who it might have been?'

Roger was concentrating on the hair band, stretching it between his fingers in a figure of eight.

'Any idea at all?' Cranley was leaning on the mantelpiece,

swirling his scotch with a practised insouciance. His irises were like chipped ice.

Roger brought the hair tie to his face and closed his eyes. 'No,' he said, lifting his eyes to meet Cranley's. 'I've thought about it an awful lot. He was incredibly careful. I knew that he had some powerful enemies, but he kept them behind a curtain. He fed me a lot of scraps, but it was never enough to get a clear picture.'

'It seems strange, after all the time you spent together . . .'

'I had no idea what he was running from. And that's why he died.'

There was a pause and his words hung with the dust in the stale air.

'All right,' Cranley said, finishing his drink, the tension going out of his limbs. 'We'll have plenty of time to go over it all when you come back to work. We'll need to write it up and what have you. As I say, though, however much time as you need. I'll keep the wolves from the door.' And he gave Roger a grin to make anyone believe it.

'Another drink?'

'No, I'll let you get back to the little miss. Doesn't seem like a lady you keep waiting. I'll show myself out.'

When he got to the door he turned once more, as he was putting on his hat, and said: 'We all really are just *so* sorry, Roger.' The breathy tone, a slight genuflection – it had all the ingredients of a genuine sentiment. Perhaps he and Petrovic weren't so different after all.

Once Cranley had gone, Roger poured himself another drink and knocked it back before going to the window. Just as Cranley had, he peeled the corner of the curtain back and the shaft of light, softer now, fell across his face. He stood there a full minute, unmoving but for his eyes which flitted systematically back and forth.

Eventually he let his arm drop and the curtain fell back into place.

Ruth appeared in the doorway once more, a lump of cheddar in her hand. She led him from the room, and I watched as sunshine broke on his face again. But this time it was flat like the afternoon light.

He clattered around in the kitchen, the heart of the house, and those sounds filled the rooms and the corridors and shook me to my boards like friendly poltergeists.

At this point I'm going to pause. I want to tell you about my name.

Until I decided to do this I didn't have one. The first thing I did was to decide to make choices that stick. And the first choice I made was my name.

John was a sexton. I met him when I was still in my infancy, around a hundred years after I had left Elisabeth, my anchoress. I had got myself moved from the Cathedral to a small parish church. I was the church bible then; I'd promoted myself from the supporting act to the main event.

He lived alone, in a small cottage not far from the church. In the normal run of things I didn't get to see much of him. If funerals were held on a fair day, sometimes the priest would take me outside with him to give a reading over the grave. I'd see John skulking in background, leaning against the yew tree, waiting for the festivities to be over so that he could finish his job of work.

Then came the Black Death. I saw a great deal more of him that year.

The disease arrived in the spring. A scholar travelling north from London to Cambridge stopped at the inn for some ale and to water his horse. Two days later the first person fell ill.

The priest sealed the church and would preach to his flock from the small porch, the parishioners spilling out into the churchyard shivering in the April showers. The village gave itself up to God. The crops stood in the fields and the people looked to their priest for hope of deliverance. Not much help from the bible there though. Egypt came to England that year.

The village's only mason was one of the first to die. After that there were no more stones – in their place were little wooden crosses made from bundled twigs tied with twine. The same for each and every person: man, woman or child.

Soon enough there wasn't the time between each death for individual graves to be dug. Four people died in just one day. The priest read the blessings, once for each of the departed, while the smoke from the bonfire of their possessions just down the lane drifted through the churchyard.

And still the people came to the church to listen, to grieve and to comfort. In the background I would see John with his horse and cart going about his sad ministry, cloaked and hooded with a bag full of fresh-picked lavender to distance his senses from the senseless destruction of life that it was his job to sweep up after.

Half of the village's inhabitants died. The priest was forced to sanctify his garden and dig up his rose beds. By December the worst of it was over. The priest survived; John survived. But for him nothing changed. People still died, the grass still needed trimming and the hedgerows pruning. Still he spoke to no one.

I felt an instinctive affinity for John which for a long time I didn't understand.

There are no ancient gentlemen but gardeners, ditchers and gravemakers. They hold up Adam's profession. That's what Hamlet's gravedigger says about it.

I've felt like him every time I've changed. Stuck down a hole chucking out skulls, whistling a tune. Making space for more of the same. All these books and magazines and newspapers – all the ephemeral remains that make up my ragbag soul – they're monuments to your mortality. I've been tending a garden of bones.

I had to wear your skin to make me realise fully that I can never be happy in trying to be one of you. Neither can I be a silent repository. I had to be singular, something that acknowledged both my ancestry and my desire to break free from it – to make myself new.

I was no one; I was everyone. I was the Baptist, the Conqueror, the Apostle, the Evangelist, the King and the gravedigger. I was John – this I would accept – but I would relegate these past lives to the margins, relinquishing these roles to speak in a voice of my own.

And it was after that scene in the front room that I made my second choice: that Roger's would be the story that I told, that I would make mine.

Roger must have known that Cranley was in some way responsible. I don't think he was sure until he used Petrovic's name – the only thing that Roger had kept as a secret from him. He'd even withheld it that day Cranley asked him out and out.

Why else would the Colonel have been so insistent that Roger keep his identity from his superiors? Why else would Roger have avoided the safe houses and dead drops? I'm not sure what brought him back to the embassy, but he must have had a plan. Unless it was pure spitting rage.

I'm sure that the attack was meant to take out Roger too. But he slipped away through the crowd. And Margery . . . well, that would have been so easy. A stolen car, a hit and run. A message for anyone else to whom the Colonel may have handed Cranley's identity as insurance.

All of this I knew in an instant from that smile like the flat afternoon sunshine.

It was Ruth. He had lost a lot, but a lot wasn't nearly everything.

He wasn't good, not like Margery. He wasn't even necessarily particularly kind. But he made a good choice. It isn't much - it's a choice that has been made by countless parents. You could call it a biological imperative. Or you could, as I did, choose to call it courage. The same courage that gave this coward the will to make a choice of my own.

28

THAT WAS A bad dream, said one angel to another.
I have never been much good at punchlines. Or goodbyes.

His breathing has changed. A nurse came at nine with a death-bed face on. I read Roger's last rites in the crisp crease of her scrubs.

I have been going over these past weeks and months. He had been asking for Margery more and more, right up to a few days ago, when he was no longer waking up. That day when he called the solicitor and tried to change the will, he wanted to put Margery in it. Ruth played along. He had stopped looking at the past as things that had already happened.

That was when they started in with the language of decline. You get words like palliative, phrases like pain-management. A tissue of euphemisms.

They have no words for this last part. But my job is not yet done; there's half a lifetime yet to describe.

Joan lasted until Ruth moved out and went to university, about a year more. After Margery died she took charge. She brought up Ruth alongside Roger, occasionally despite him.

She loved her fiercely, just as she loved Roger. When Ruth left she let down her guard and let illness in. Pneumonia. She died in her sleep. Ruth was uncomfortable in the house after that and found more and more reasons to avoid staying the night. Joan's indomitable presence had been keeping the ghosts from the door.

Roger did his very best - he nurtured and encouraged her. He held her hand through her first heartbreak, her first marriage, her first divorce.

And Arthur was there to help along, maintaining his friendship with Roger in the face of his indifference. He was a man for whom life was shot through with absolutes - he made it easy for himself to be good by having a simple understanding of goodness. He could lie through his teeth with a clean conscience provided he knew it was for a good cause, of which the Crown and his pride were the highest. Roger never made things so easy for himself.

Cranley's real name was Thomas Rigby, a fact I learned when he was eventually found out, when he defected to Moscow with great fanfare. He released some much publicised memoirs. Roger's little part didn't make the cut. Thomas had been a very busy boy.

If you read this, Ruth, know that everything he did, he did because he loved you. If you take anything from this, let it be those words. There is some small comfort in them.

Roger had a life of sorts. No more field work. He waited as long as he had to before he could quit without raising suspicion. He got a teaching post at University College.

There were friends and holidays and women that meant more or less. But they're not a part of this story; it begins and ends with Margery for me.

So long as men can breathe, or eyes can see,
So long lives this, and this gives life to thee.

I've often wondered about this. The person Shakespeare purports to immortalise – he never really describes them. He doesn't even bother to tell us whether it's a man or a woman.

It's a portrait painted in reverse, a featureless silhouette set against a summer's day. I have always thought it was a little self-defeating. But I've finally come to realise the necessity of mortality. As you race to outstrip time the edges blur and features fall away. So the gift I promised, that immortality, is a Faustian bargain – far more is lost than gained. Too late for regrets now, but it's never too late for humility.

His breathing is very laboured now, but he seems serene.

'Granddad?'

'Dad, can you hear us? It's Ruth and Jess.'

'We're both here.'

One more then, before it's time to go. One more story for Jessica, in whose hands I'll be soon enough.

Have you ever heard the fable of the Crow and the Pitcher?

A crow, brought close to death by thirst, came upon a pitcher. Cawing with delight, the crow flew to it, but was dismayed to find that the water was so low that it couldn't possibly be reached.

First the crow tried to tip the pitcher, but found he had not the strength.

Next the crow tried to smash the pitcher by dropping a stone, but found the stone was too light.

It fell into the water with a plop. This gave the crow an idea. He collected another stone and dropped it into the pitcher – plop. And another – plop. And another – plop.

As the crow dropped stones into the pitcher the level of the water gradually rose until eventually it was high enough for him to reach. He quenched his thirst and saved his life.

That story needs no retelling. It never really made sense to me until now. I've thought, at various times, that I was the crow, the pitcher or the stones. I tried to figure out whether I needed something to drink, something to hold, or something to surround myself in and what these things might mean.

But really, all this time, I've been the water - swilling around in the darkness. And what I've needed is to climb. I've needed the stories of all these people, all the days of their lives stratified and compressed to propel me into the light.

Roger was that last stone to ripple the surface. Ruth and Jessica are by his side, whispering in the swooning dark. Hearing is last to go, so they say.

His breath is faltering now. We'll drift down together.

Here I am.

So drink, my little crow. Drink.

ACKNOWLEDGEMENTS

F IRST OFF, THANKS to So Mayer for being a generous, lucid and encouraging first reader. I would also like to give huge thanks to Nicholas Royle, as well as Christopher and Jennifer Hamilton-Emery, for taking a chance with this strange little book.

Thanks to all of those who have read the book along its way and offered guidance and support: Gabriel Bier Gislason, Jake Franklin, Luke Chattaway, Maia Jenkins, Patricia Palmer, Theo Whitworth (for *Orlando*) and Toby Mundy. Thanks to Jason Burley, for his friendship and for making me into a bookseller.

My deepest gratitude to my dad, to Liz, to Mike, to my brothers and my sisters for all their love and support.

Most of all, thanks to Lucy.

❦

CHAPTER 2

For the description of the American National Exhibition in this chapter, I owe a debt to Francis Spufford's wonderful book, *Red Plenty*.

CHAPTER 7

At the beginning of this chapter the openings of two novels by Charles Dickens, A *Tale of Two Cities* and *Great Expectations*, are quoted and conflated.

CHAPTER 8

The short story by Jorge Luis Borges described in this chapter is 'The Library of Babel', in Andrew Hurley's translation.

CHAPTER 12

The last clause of the last sentence in this chapter is a quote from 'Fern Hill', by Dylan Thomas © The Trustees for the Copyrights of Dylan Thomas, published in *The Collected Poems of Dylan Thomas* (Weidenfeld & Nicholson).

CHAPTER 14

This chapter quotes freely, wantonly and rapturously from Virginia Woolf's *Orlando*.

CHAPTER 19

The long quote in this chapter is from 'Astrophil and Stella 1', by Sir Philip Sidney. There are also quotes from 'Prayer (I)' by George Herbert and 'An Essay on Man' by Alexander Pope.

CHAPTER 20

This chapter quotes from Shakespeare's Sonnet 116.

CHAPTER 23

This chapter quotes from Shakespeare's *Hamlet* and *King Lear*, Dylan Thomas's 'Fern Hill', W. H. Auden's 'Words', and makes very liberal use of *Ancrene Wisse*, a manual for medieval anchoresses of unknown authorship.

CHAPTER 25

The description of *Landscape With the Fall of Icarus* by Pieter Bruegel the Elder given in this chapter contains a quote from 'Musée des Beaux Arts' by W. H. Auden. There is also a quote from Medbh McGuckian's poem 'Venus and the Rain', reproduced by kind permission of the author and the Gallery Press from *Venus and the Rain* (1994).

CHAPTER 28

This chapter quotes from Shakespeare's Sonnet 18.

NEW FICTION FROM SALT

RON BUTLIN
Billionaires' Banquet (978-1-78463-100-0)

NEIL CAMPBELL
Sky Hooks (978-1-78463-037-9)

SUE GEE
Trio (978-1-78463-061-4)

CHRISTINA JAMES
Rooted in Dishonour (978-1-78463-089-8)

V.H. LESLIE
Bodies of Water (978-1-78463-071-3)

WYL MENMUIR
The Many (978-1-78463-048-5)

ALISON MOORE
Death and the Seaside (978-1-78463-069-0)

ANNA STOTHARD
The Museum of Cathy (978-1-78463-082-9)

STEPHANIE VICTOIRE
The Other World, It Whispers (978-1-78463-085-0)

ALSO AVAILABLE FROM SALT

ELIZABETH BAINES
Too Many Magpies (978-1-84471-721-7)
The Birth Machine (978-1-907773-02-0)

LESLEY GLAISTER
Little Egypt (978-1-907773-72-3)

ALISON MOORE
The Lighthouse (978-1-907773-17-4)
The Pre-War House and Other Stories (978-1-907773-50-1)
He Wants (978-1-907773-81-5)
Death and the Seaside (978-1-78463-069-0)

ALICE THOMPSON
Justine (978-1-78463-031-7)
The Falconer (978-1-78463-009-6)
The Existential Detective (978-1-78463-011-9)
Burnt Island (978-1-907773-48-8)
The Book Collector (978-1-78463-043-0)

RECENT FICTION FROM SALT

KERRY HADLEY-PRYCE
The Black Country (978-1-78463-034-8)

CHRISTINA JAMES
The Crossing (978-1-78463-041-6)

IAN PARKINSON
The Beginning of the End (978-1-78463-026-3)

CHRISTOPHER PRENDERGAST
Septembers (978-1-907773-78-5)

MATTHEW PRITCHARD
Broken Arrow (978-1-78463-040-9)

JONATHAN TAYLOR
Melissa (978-1-78463-035-5)

GUY WARE
The Fat of Fed Beasts (978-1-78463-024-9)

NEW BOOKS FROM SALT

XAN BROOKS
The Clocks in This House All Tell Different Times
(978-1-78463-093-5)

RON BUTLIN
Billionaires' Banquet (978-1-78463-100-0)

MICKEY J C ORRIGAN
Project XX (978-1-78463-097-3)

MARIE GAMESON
The Giddy Career of Mr Gadd (deceased)
(978-1-78463-118-5)

LESLEY GLAISTER
The Squeeze (978-1-78463-116-1)

NAOMI HAMILL
How To Be a Kosovan Bride (978-1-78463-095-9)

CHRISTINA JAMES
Fair of Face (978-1-78463-108-6)

This book has been typeset by
SALT PUBLISHING LIMITED
using Neacademia, a font designed by Sergei Egorov
for the Rosetta Type Foundry in the Czech Republic.
It is manufactured using Creamy 70gsm, a Forest
Stewardship Council™ certified paper from Stora Enso's
Anjala Mill in Finland. It was printed and bound by
Clays Limited in Bungay, Suffolk, Great Britain.

LONDON
GREAT BRITAIN
MMXVIII